Note from the Publisher

More than a million fans have read the epic battle of good versus evil within the Circle Series (*Green, Black, Red, White*) and the Lost series for young adults (*Chosen, Infidel, Renegade, Chaos, Lunatic* and *Elyon*). Yes— many have read these series. But far fewer have ever SEEN the scenes visually brought to life through hundreds of full-color illustrations.

As both a fan and the publisher of these series, it brings me great joy to present to you *The Circle Series Visual Edition*. For the first time ever, we've brought the full-color graphic novels of *Black, Red* and *White* (previously available only individually) together in a single high-quality hardcover binding.

If you've already read these novels, this will be an exciting new way to dive even deeper into the adrenaline-laced series. For those new to the Circle universe, this is a fantastic introduction to a fantastical epic that will live with you long after the last page.

Welcome to the Circle. In Living Color.

BLACK

THE BIRTH OF EVIL

11:08 PM - DENVER COLORADO

ONE OF THE BENEFITS OF THE LAST SHIFT AT THE JAVA HUT: FREE CAFFEINE...

SMACK!

HUH?

WHAT THE...?

THAT'S WEIRD...

SMACK!

SOMEBODY'S SHOOTING AT ME!

NOT BAD FOR AN OUT OF SHAPE BLUE BELT.

IF THEY FOUND OUT WHERE I WORK THEN THEY KNOW WHERE I LIVE.

UNGHHH

HEAD'S THROBBING NOW.

GOTTA GET OFF THE STREETS. KARA'S PLACE SHOULD BE SAFE.

SHE CAN FIX ME UP WHEN SHE FINISHES HER SHIFT AT THE ER.

ANYWAY, SHE'S ALWAYS COMPLAINING HER LITTLE BROTHER DOESN'T VISIT ENOUGH.

LOOKS ALL CLEAR. THINK I'M SAFE. FOR THE MOMENT AT LEAST.

GOOD THING I KNOW WHERE SHE KEEPS HER SPARE KEY.

MAYBE I SHOULD LIE DOWN... JUST FOR A MINUTE.

KARA WILL BE HOME SOON...

... SHE CAN TELL ME...

...IF IT'S SERIOUS...

WHAT... WHAT IS THIS?

OH DEAR, HIS WOUNDS ARE HORRIBLE!

HOW COULD ANYTHING LIKE THIS POSSIBLY HAVE HAPPENED?

THE SHATAIKI! RACHELLE, I LED HIM FROM THE BLACK FOREST.

WHAT? HE'S BEEN *IN* THE BLACK FOREST?

YES, BUT HE DIDN'T DRINK THE WATER.

THIS IS WHY TANIS HAS TALKED ABOUT AN EXPEDITION TO DESTROY THOSE BLACK BATS!

THEY'RE EVIL!

HIS TALK IS FOOLISH, RACHELLE. ANY SUCH EXPEDITION WOULD PUT TANIS IN THE SAME CONDITION!

THE WATER PLEASE, GABIL.

...WAIT.

WAIT? IS HE... DO YOU THINK HE'S MARKED?

WHAT DO YOU MEAN?

UNDER THE BLOOD ON HIS FOREHEAD...

DOES HE BEAR THE MARK OF UNION?

IT'S A WONDERFUL IDEA! HOW UTTERLY ROMANTIC!

YOU CAN'T BE SERIOUSLY THINKING ABOUT...

WHY NOT?

YOU DON'T EVEN KNOW HIM!

SINCE WHEN HAS THAT EVER MADE ANY DIFFERENCE TO ANY WOMAN?

DOES ELYON EXERCISE SUCH DISCRIMINATION?

WHAT YOU'RE FEELING IS EMPATHY, NOT...

DON'T BE SO QUICK TO DECIDE WHAT I'M FEELING.

HE HAS BEEN THROUGH THE MOST AWFUL ORDEAL IMAGINABLE, BUT...

NO, IT'S NOT THE WORST IMAGINABLE. TRUST ME.

GABIL UNDERSTANDS. I FEEL SOMETHING FOR THIS MAN. I FOUND HIM, MAYBE I'M MEANT TO CHOOSE HIM.

THAT'S NOT SO UNREASONABLE, IS IT?

NO, I DON'T THINK SO.

HE'S PROBABLY ALREADY MARKED ANYWAY...

THEN I SUPPOSE THERE'S ONE WAY TO FIND OUT.

THERE'S NO MARK!

PERFECT!

IT'S YOUR CHOICE, I SUPPOSE.

WOULD YOU LIKE TO BRING HIM WHOLENESS?

I WOULD.

GASP!

WHERE AM I?

YOU CAME FROM THE BLACK FOREST. DON'T WORRY, YOU DIDN'T DRINK THE WATER.

I AM MICHAL AND THIS IS GABIL.

AND I'M RACHELLE.

HOW DO YOU FEEL?

MY WOUNDS... THEY'RE GONE!

I FEEL... FINE.

A LITTLE GROGGY. AM I DREAMING AGAIN?

OR IS THIS REAL?

WHAT IS YOUR NAME?

ERM... THOMAS HUNTER?

YOU ARE A BEAUTIFUL MAN, THOMAS HUNTER.

I HAVE CHOSEN YOU.

WHAT? WAIT!

ARE YOU HURT? IS THAT BLOOD?

KARA... WE'VE GOT A PROBLEM.

THAT'S FUNNY. THE BACK OF MY HEAD DOESN'T HURT ANYMORE.

BUT I WAS SHOT THERE... WASN'T I?

WHAT'S WRONG? I DON'T SEE ANYTHING, YOU'RE FINE!

LISTEN, YOU KNOW HOW MOM WAS IN DEBT?

A FEW YEARS AGO, I... BORROWED SOME MONEY TO HELP HER PAY IT OFF.

THOMAS... DON'T TELL ME YOU GOT MIXED UP WITH THOSE CROOKS FROM NEW YORK.

HOW MUCH?

ONE HUNDRED THOUSAND.

ONE HUNDRED THOUSAND DOLLARS?! HOW ON EARTH...?

IT'S A LONG STORY, BUT BASICALLY I CONVINCED THEM I WAS AN ARMS DEALER.

THAT'S NOT IMPORTANT NOW.

LISTEN, KARA... THEY FOUND ME TONIGHT, AND THEY SHOT AT ME.

A BULLET GRAZED THE BACK OF MY HEAD. NOTHING FATAL, BUT IT WAS MESSY.

BUT THEN, I HAD THIS CRAZY DREAM, AND...

WELL, EVERYTHING'S *FINE* NOW. I'M NOT FEELING A THING.

WAIT A MINUTE. THINGS ARE MAKING SENSE NOW.

I KNOW WHAT'S GOING ON...

YOU'VE GOT TO BE KIDDING ME, THOMAS.

WHAT DID YOU DO? TAKE TOO MUCH PAIN MEDICATION?

OR IS THIS JUST ANOTHER STORY YOU'RE WRITING?

NO, KARA, DON'T YOU SEE?

THIS IS A DREAM. IT ALL MAKES SENSE NOW.

THE BLACK FOREST, THE BATS, MICHAL, RACHELLE... THAT'S REAL.

I GOT HURT, I HIT MY HEAD, AND I'M SLEEPING IT OFF AND *THIS* IS A DREAM.

SURE, THOMAS. WHATEVER.

NO, KARA, WAIT...

HUH?

THE RAISON VACCINE?

RAISON VACCINE

THIS IS BAD! MICHAL TOLD ME ABOUT THIS...

THIS IS THE VACCINE THAT WILL START...

...THE END OF THE WORLD.

WHO'S MICHAL??

HE'S LIKE... A WHITE OWL, WITH GREEN EYES. LISTEN, KARA. WE NEED TO WARN PEOPLE.

ABOUT WHAT?

THIS VACCINE TURNS INTO A VIRUS. AT THE BEGINNING OF THE TWENTY-FIRST CENTURY. JUST LIKE THEY SAID.

FIRST I'M A DREAM, AND NOW YOU'RE A PROPHET?

GO BACK TO SLEEP, THOMAS. MAYBE YOU'LL MAKE MORE SENSE IN THE MORNING.

KARA, I'M TELLING YOU... MICHAL WARNED ME. THEY CALL OUR WORLD "THE HISTORIES."

HOW CAN I PROVE THIS TO YOU?

THE KENTUCKY DERBY'S RUNNING TODAY. AND YOU DON'T KNOW ANYTHING ABOUT HORSE RACING.

SO WHY DON'T YOU GO BACK TO THE FUTURE AND ASK YOUR OWL FRIEND WHO WON. THAT SHOULD PROVE IT'S ALL IN YOUR HEAD.

NOW GO GET SOME SLEEP.

I'M TELLING YOU, I DON'T KNOW ANYTHING!

I DON'T KNOW ANYTHING ABOUT THAT BLACK FOREST, OR THAT WEIRD WATER, OR THAT WOMAN WHO HEALED ME...

DID SHE SAY SHE'S CHOSEN ME? WHAT DOES THAT EVEN MEAN?

DEAR, DEAR. THIS SHOULD BE INTERESTING. RACHELLE HAS CHOSEN A MAN WITH NO MEMORY.

HOW ROMANTIC!

I AM WHAT THEY CALL A WISE ONE - THE ONLY WISE ONE IN THIS PART OF THE FOREST. I HAVE A PERFECT MEMORY.

I'LL DO MY BEST TO EXPLAIN THINGS.

THAT IS THE BLACK FOREST. DO YOU REMEMBER IT?

OF COURSE. I WAS IN IT, REMEMBER?

I JUST THOUGHT I WOULD MAKE SURE. THAT FOREST IS WHERE THE SHATAIKI LIVE.

AND THAT RIVER RUNS AROUND THE WHOLE PLANET, DIVIDING THE BLACK FOREST FROM THE GREEN - EVIL FROM GOOD.

THE RIVER RUNS TOO FAST TO SWIM ACROSS - THE ONLY WAY TO CROSS IS ACROSS ONE OF THE BRIDGES.

YOU COULD NOT HAVE COME FROM THIS PART OF THE GREEN FOREST - I WOULD HAVE KNOWN YOU, SINCE THIS AREA IS IN MY CHARGE.

I CAN ONLY ASSUME YOU ENTERED INTO THE BLACK FOREST AT ONE OF THE OTHER CROSSINGS AND MADE YOUR WAY HERE.

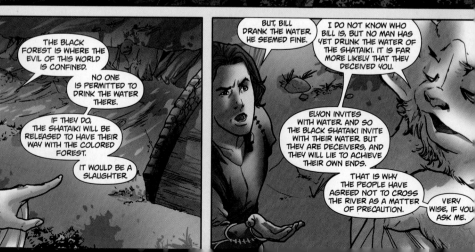

THE BLACK FOREST IS WHERE THE EVIL OF THIS WORLD IS CONFINED.

NO ONE IS PERMITTED TO DRINK THE WATER THERE.

IF THEY DO, THE SHATAIKI WILL BE RELEASED TO HAVE THEIR WAY WITH THE COLORED FOREST.

IT WOULD BE A SLAUGHTER.

BUT, BILL DRANK THE WATER. HE SEEMED FINE.

I DO NOT KNOW WHO BILL IS, BUT NO MAN HAS YET DRUNK THE WATER OF THE SHATAIKI. IT IS FAR MORE LIKELY THAT THEY DECEIVED YOU.

ELYON INVITES WITH WATER AND SO THE BLACK SHATAIKI INVITE WITH THEIR WATER. BUT THEY ARE DECEIVERS, AND THEY WILL LIE TO ACHIEVE THEIR OWN ENDS.

THAT IS WHY THE PEOPLE HAVE AGREED NOT TO CROSS THE RIVER AS A MATTER OF PRECAUTION.

VERY WISE, IF YOU ASK ME.

IT'S AMAZING...

WHA-?

SOMETHING TINGLING, UP MY ARM...

IT'S QUITE ALL RIGHT, MY FRIEND. MADE FROM A THOUSAND GREEN TREES.

NOT A BLEMISH TO BE FOUND. IT'S PERFECT, JUST LIKE ELYON.

IT'S .. LIKE THE WATER?

NO, NO, THE WATER IS SPECIAL. BUT ELYON IS THE MAKER OF BOTH.

I MUST BE OFF NOW, DUTY CALLS. I WILL LEAVE YOU HERE. RACHELLE WILL BE HERE SHORTLY TO PICK YOU UP, AFTER THE GATHERING. REMEMBER...WHEN IN DOUBT—JUST PLAY ALONG.

RIGHT.

I JUST HOPE SHE HASN'T BITTEN OFF MORE THAN SHE CAN CHEW...

JUST PLAY ALONG, HE SAYS.

IT'S EXHAUSTING TO TRY AND FIGURE THIS ALL OUT.

JUST PLAY ALONG...

THAT'S IT, COME ON. WAKE UP.

YOU FEEL OK?

I GETTHHH.

I GUESS.

SO?

DID YOU DREAM?

I DON'T KNOW, AM I DREAMING NOW? AM I SLEEPING NOW?

JOY FLYER. THE HORSE THAT WON THE KENTUCKY DERBY. JOY FLYER.

HMMM...

NOT YET, HE HASN'T. HE'S A LONG SHOT. HOW DID YOU EVEN KNOW THAT NAME?

I TOLD YOU, I DIDN'T. MICHAL TOLD ME IN MY DREAMS.

SO YOU'RE TELLING ME YOU'RE GETTING FACTS IN YOUR DREAMS ABOUT THE FUTURE AS IF THEY'RE HISTORY?!

HOW LONG WERE YOU THERE?

I'M NOT SURE. 5 OR 6 HOURS?

YOU WERE ONLY ASLEEP FOR HALF AN HOUR TOPS.

DID YOU FIND OUT MORE ABOUT THE RAISON STRAIN?

NO... I DIDN'T ASK ANYTHING ABOUT---

---YOU SHOULD HAVE. WE NEED TO CALL SOMEONE ABOUT THIS.

WHO?

15 MINUTES LATER...

THE CENTER FOR DISEASE CONTROL DOESN'T SEEM INTERESTED. THEY THINK WE'RE KOOKS.

HAND ME THE PHONE. I HAVE AN IDEA.

BUREAU FOR INTERNATIONAL NARCOTICS AND LAW ENFORCEMENT AFFAIRS, BOB MACKLROY..

HELLO, BOB. LISTEN. THOMAS HUNTER HERE. I HAVE INFORMATION ABOUT A SERIOUS THREAT TO THIS COUNTRY.

THREAT? WHAT KIND?

A VIRUS.

DO YOU HAVE THE NUMBER FOR THE CDC?

ACTUALLY, WE ALREADY TRIED THEM AND THEY SORT OF BLEW US OFF.

LOOK, SIR, I KNOW THIS SOUNDS STRANGE, AND YOU HAVE NO CLUE WHO WE ARE, BUT YOU HAVE TO HEAR ME OUT...

HAVE YOU EVER HEARD OF THE RAISON VACCINE?

...IT'S AN AIRBORNE VACCINE ABOUT TO HIT THE MARKET WHICH WILL MUTATE UNDER EXTREME HEAT...NO, I SAW IT IN MY DREAM...YOU HAVE TO BELIEVE ME...

I HAVE TO ADMIT, MR. HUNTER WHAT YOU'VE JUST TOLD ME IS INDEED... CURIOUS.

I KNOW IT ALL SOUNDS STRANGE. BUT YOU CAN'T IGNORE THIS. THE VACCINE CAN OR WILL MUTATE UNDER EXTREME HEAT AND WIPE OUT... EVERYONE. YOU HAVE TO CONSIDER THE FACTS HERE.

OH, I AM MR. HUNTER, AND THAT'S WHAT'S TROUBLING ME. ARE YOU ACTUALLY TELLING ME THAT ALL THIS INFORMATION CAME...FROM A DREAM?

YOU SAY THAT LIKE IT'S PREPOSTEROUS! DID YOU HEAR A WORD OF WHAT HE JUST TOLD YOU? HE KNOWS ABOUT THE RAISON VACCINE...HE KNEW ABOUT IT BEFORE IT WAS MADE PUBLIC!

WELL...THE RAISON VACCINE HAS BEEN TOUTED IN PRIVATE CIRCLES FOR A FEW MONTHS NOW----

NOT IN HIS PRIVATE CIRCLES.

THE WINNER OF THE KENTUCKY DERBY WASN'T PUBLIC TWO HOURS AGO WHEN I PLACED MY BET.

EXPLAIN HOW THOMAS JUST WON ME $345,000 DOLLARS ON A HUNCH FROM THE SAME DREAMS!

YOU WHA-?

I DON'T KNOW THAT YOU BET ON JOY FLYER. I CAN'T BE CERTAIN YOU DON'T HAVE STOCK IN RAISON PHARMACEUTICAL'S COMPETITOR AND ARE LOOKING TO TRASH RAISON. I CAN'T DO A THING WITH THIS EXCEPT PUT IT THROUGH THE NORMAL CHANNELS.

SO YOU'RE GOING TO DISMISS IT? JUST LIKE THAT?

NO, I SAID I'D REPORT IT--I SUGGEST YOU GO COLLECT YOUR WINNINGS.

YOU'RE LATE.

I WAS DELAYED. WHY DID YOU CALL ME?

I NEED YOU TO INTERVIEW MONIQUE DE RAISON.

THE RAISON VACCINE? I WASN'T AWARE THEIR VACCINE HELD ANY PROMISE FOR US.

OUR CONTACT SAID THE RUMORS OF THE MUTATIONS COULD BE TRUE.

RUMORS...

THEY WERE BROUGHT TO OUR ATTENTION BY A MAN NAMED THOMAS HUNTER

THE DREAMER? NOW WE'RE RESORTING TO MYSTICS?

HE KNOWS THINGS HE SHOULDN'T. AND I WANT TO KNOW WHY.

I'M NOT SURE MS. DE RAISON WILL OFFER AN... INTERVIEW.

THEN YOU WILL PERSUADE HER TO COOPERATE.

AND HUNTER?

LEARN EVERYTHING HE KNOWS...

THEN KILL HIM.

WHERE AM I? OH... RIGHT. THE HOME OF RACHELLE'S FAMILY.

THOMAS!

DO YOU WANT TO PLAY, THOMAS?

PLAY? UM, LISTEN, UH... JOHAN, RIGHT? I HAVE TO FIND MY VILLAGE.

THEN YOU NEED TO GO SEE TANIS, HE'LL HELP YOU FIND YOUR VILLAGE. HE'S WAITING FOR YOU WITH MY FATHER

YOUR FATHER? ...WITH RACHELLE?

HMM, SO YOU WANT TO SEE RACHELLE?

UH, NOT NECESSARILY. JUST WONDERED IF...

OH, SHE WANTS TO SEE YOU! IT'S VERY EXCITING, DON'T YOU THINK?

IS HE SAYING WHAT I THINK HE'S SAYING? DOES THE WHOLE VILLAGE KNOW ABOUT US?

THEY SAID YOU HIT YOUR HEAD AND LOST YOUR MEMORY. IS THAT FUN?

NOT ESPECIALLY.

WELL THEN COME WITH ME! COME ON—THEY'RE WAITING FOR YOU. YOU'LL HAVE FUN!

WHAT'S HE DOING?

YOU DON'T REMEMBER?

HE'S MAKING A LADLE. MAYBE A GIFT FOR SOMEONE.

THAT'S INCREDIBLE.

HE'S SCULPTING THAT WOOD LIKE IT'S CLAY!

NO, I GUESS I DON'T REMEMBER

OH THIS IS AMAZING! YOU REALLY DON'T REMEMBER ALL THIS! YOU ARE GOING TO LOVE THE STORYTELLERS.

HERE, I HAVE SOMETHING FOR YOU.

KEEP THIS. MAYBE IT WILL HELP YOU REMEMBER

THANK YOU, I HOPE IT DOES.

COME. LET'S FIND TANIS!

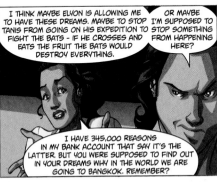

DID YOU HEAR WHAT SHE JUST SAID?

HUH? NO.

THEY'RE STILL WAITING FOR FDA APPROVAL IN THE US, BUT SEVEN COUNTRIES IN AFRICA AND THREE IN ASIA HAVE ALREADY PLACED ORDERS FOR THE VACCINE!

THE FIRST ORDER IS GOING TO SOUTH AFRICA IN TWENTY-FOUR HOURS!

....NOW, I'LL BE HAPPY TO ANSWER A FEW QUESTIONS.

WE HAVE TO STOP THAT SHIPMENT!

SHE SAID SHE'D TALK TO US AFTERWARDS.

WHAT IF SHE WON'T LISTEN?

THEN WE TRY THE AUTHORITIES. RIGHT?

RIGHT, THOMAS?

RIGHT.

WHAT DOES THAT MEAN?

IT MEANS... RIGHT.

I DON'T LIKE THE WAY YOU SAID---

LET'S GO.

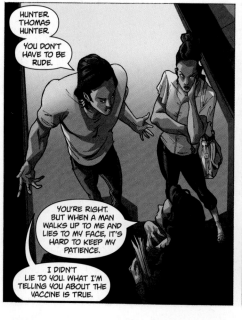

HUH?

OOMPH!

AAAH!

I'M SORRY, BUT YOU *HAVE* TO LISTEN TO ME.

PLEASE, MR. HUNTER. GET A HOLD OF YOURSELF.

I WON'T KILL YOU.

PUT YOUR GUNS DOWN, YOU IDIOTS! ONE MOVE AND I SHOOT HER

AND I WANT ANOTHER HOSTAGE- YOU THERE IN THE YELLOW SHIRT, COME HERE *NOW!*

GET THE DOOR.

ANYONE WHO FOLLOWS US, ANY POLICE OR ANY AUTHORITIES AND BOTH THESE LOVELY LADIES ARE DEAD!

30 MINUTES LATER. THE PARADISE HOTEL.

SOME PARADISE, THIS PLACE IS A DUMP!

I GOT US A SUITE.

OKAY. LET'S GO, AND WE GO QUIET. I MEANT IT WHEN I SAID I WOULDN'T KILL YOU.

BUT I MIGHT PUT A BULLET IN YOUR PINKIE TOE IF YOUR BEHAVIOR REQUIRES IT. WE CLEAR?

I'LL TAKE YOUR SILENCE AS AGREEMENT. LET'S GO.

TOP FLOOR

I DON'T KNOW IF I CAN DO THIS, TOM.

YOU'RE NOT DOING THIS. I AM. I'M THE ONE HAVING THE DREAMS. I'M THE ONE WHO KNOWS WHAT I SHOULDN'T. THAT'S WHY I NEED TO TALK SOME SENSE INTO THIS SPOILED BRAT.

WHAT IS IT WITH YOU FRENCH, ANYWAY? ALWAYS BUSINESS BEFORE SAVING THE WORLD?

THIS FROM THE MAN WITH THE GUN IN MY BACK?

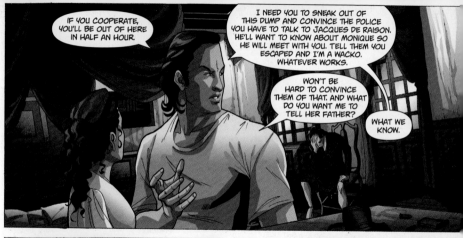

IF YOU COOPERATE, YOU'LL BE OUT OF HERE IN HALF AN HOUR.

I NEED YOU TO SNEAK OUT OF THIS DUMP AND CONVINCE THE POLICE YOU HAVE TO TALK TO JACQUES DE RAISON. HE'LL WANT TO KNOW ABOUT MONIQUE SO HE WILL MEET WITH YOU. TELL THEM YOU ESCAPED AND I'M A WACKO. WHATEVER WORKS.

WON'T BE HARD TO CONVINCE THEM OF THAT. AND WHAT DO YOU WANT ME TO TELL HER FATHER?

WHAT WE KNOW.

AND TELL HIM IF HE DOESN'T AGREE TO STOP OR RECALL THE SHIPMENT THAT I'M GOING TO START SHOOTING.

ONLY PINKIES, OF COURSE.

THIS IS NUTS. I HOPE YOU KNOW WHAT YOU'RE DOING.

GOOD LUCK WOOING THAT ONE, BY THE WAY.

FARTHEST THING FROM MY MIND.

CARLOS.

HOW CONVENIENT. THE TWO BIRDS I'M LOOKING FOR IN THE SAME NEST.

THOMAS?

CAN WE TALK, ON MY LEVEL, JUST FOR A MOMENT?

WHAT DO YOU THINK I'VE BEEN TRYING TO DO FOR THE PAST TWO HOURS?

YOU'VE BEEN TALKING ON *YOUR* LEVEL.

EVERYTHING YOU'RE TELLING ME, MIGHT MAKE PERFECT SENSE TO YOU, BUT NOT TO ME.

LOOK, THE VACCINE IS MOST LIKELY IN FLIGHT BY NOW AND WITHIN 48 HOURS IT WILL BE IN THE HANDS OF HUNDREDS OF HOSPITALS AROUND THE WORLD. IF YOU'RE RIGHT, WE'RE WASTING TIME JUST SITTING HERE.

THEN YOU'LL RECALL THE SHIPMENTS?

WOULD YOU BELIEVE ME IF I SAID YES?

NO.

IF I MADE THAT CALL, THE COMPANY MY FATHER AND I HAVE SPENT OUR LIVES BUILDING WOULD VERY LIKELY BE DESTROYED IN THE MATTER OF A FEW DAYS. SO FOR ME TO MAKE THAT KIND OF DECISION I'D HAVE TO BE 100% SURE THAT WHAT YOU'RE SAYING IS TRUE.

I DON'T KNOW HOW I CAN BE CLEARER. EITHER YOU BELIEVE ME OR YOU DON'T.

YOU DON'T. SO WE HAVE A PROBLEM.

YOU STILL AREN'T SPEAKING TO ME ON MY LEVEL.

I'M TRYING TO EXPLAIN MY PREDICAMENT SO YOU CAN ADDRESS ME AS A REAL PERSON. A WOMAN WHO IS... CONFUSED AND FRIGHTENED BY YOUR ANTICS.

OH, OF COURSE! YOU'RE THE ONE WHO'S FRIGHTENED.

I'M THE ONE OBSESSED WITH BATS AND FORESTS AND TRYING TO SAVE THE WORLD FROM DEVASTATION BY A NON-EXISTENT DEADLY VIRUS...

THIS IS CRAZY!

WELL, YOU SAID THAT, NOT ME. LISTEN, I'M A LOGICAL PERSON, I HAVE A PH.D. IN BIOCHEMISTRY. YOU REALLY WANT ME TO BELIEVE SOME CRAZY DREAM OF YOURS?

I DO.

THOSE CRAZY BATS KNEW YOUR NAME.

OK, LET'S TRY A DIFFERENT APPROACH. TELL ME ABOUT THE VACCINE.

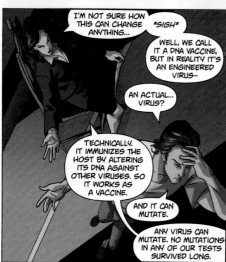

I'M NOT SURE HOW THIS CAN CHANGE ANYTHING...

SIGH

WELL, WE CALL IT A DNA VACCINE, BUT IN REALITY IT'S AN ENGINEERED VIRUS—

AN ACTUAL... VIRUS?

TECHNICALLY. IT IMMUNIZES THE HOST BY ALTERING ITS DNA AGAINST OTHER VIRUSES. SO IT WORKS AS A VACCINE.

AND IT CAN MUTATE.

ANY VIRUS CAN MUTATE. NO MUTATIONS IN ANY OF OUR TESTS SURVIVED LONG.

HMM... I JUST HAD AN IDEA.

I THINK I CAN PROVE THESE DREAMS OF MINE. ASK ME SOMETHING THAT I COULD NEVER KNOW THE ANSWER TO.

WHY?

BECAUSE I'M GOING TO FIND OUT THE ANSWER IN MY SLEEP.

NOW ASK ME SOMETHING, SOMETHING ABOUT THE VACCINE THAT ONLY YOU KNOW THE ANSWER TO.

THIS IS RIDICULOUS...

THIS IS THE ONLY WAY WE CAN RESOLVE THIS. IF I'M WRONG I PROMISE I'LL LET YOU GO.

THIS JUST GETS CRAZIER...

MONIQUE!

OKAY, OKAY! HOW MANY NUCLEOTIDE BASE PAIRS SPECIFICALLY DEAL WITH HIV IN MY VACCINE?

FINE. IN HALF AN HOUR...KICK ME UP TO WAKE ME UP. AND DON'T TRY ANYTHING IF YOU WANT TO KEEP YOUR PINKIE TOES.

CAREFUL HUNTER.

IT SEEMS QUIET...

...MAYBE TOO QUIET.

HERE WE GO.

GET IN, GET THE INFO, AND GET OUT.

HELLO THOMAS.

WELCOME TO MY WORLD. I HAD HOPED YOU WOULD COME.

I KNOW THIS MUST SEEM A LITTLE OVERWHELMING TO YOU. PLEASE, IGNORE THEM. THEY ARE MINDLESS IMBECILES.

SICK, DEMENTED CREATURES.

TAKE HIM TO SAFETY —NOW!

I ALMOST TOOK A BITE, BILL WARNED ME!

COULD... BILL BE REAL?

THOMASS..... HELP ME....

AS YOU CAN SEE, BILL IS INDEED REAL. I MUST KEEP HIM THOUGH, YOU UNDERSTAND.

IT'S THE ONE ASSURANCE I HAVE THAT YOU WILL RETURN WITH TANIS.

I PROMISE YOU, WHEN YOU RETURN, I WILL TAKE YOU BOTH BACK TO YOUR SHIP AND HELP YOU TO RETURN HOME.

I THINK IT'S TIME TO GET OUT OF HERE. BUT BILL...

THOMAS! RUN!!

HISSSSSS!

GET THAT ROUSH!

NOW HUNTER, GO!

THEY LIE, THOMAS! COME BACK AND I WILL SHOW YOU LIFE!

HAVE YOU LOST YOUR MIND?

I NEEDED INFORMATION.

WHAT INFORMATION COULD BE WORTH RISKING YOUR LIFE?

FOR MY DREAMS...

COME, FOLLOW ME! IT'S TIME.

TIME FOR WHAT?

MICHAL, DID YOU SEE HIM?

I SAW. HE IS TRULY EVIL.

NO, BILL. DID YOU SEE HIM? TEELEH SAID HE WAS MY CO-PILOT.

IS THAT WHAT THAT MONSTER TOLD YOU?

I SAW HIM, MICHAL. *YOU* SAW HIM!

I WILL TELL YOU WHAT I SAW, THOMAS.

I SAW NOTHING BUT LIES.

TEELEH WOULD TELL YOU ANYTHING TO LURE YOU INTO HIS TRAP.

BUT IF BILL IS REAL--

BILL ISN'T REAL! WHAT YOU SAW WAS A FIGMENT OF YOUR IMAGINATION! A CREATION OF THAT MONSTER!

BUT BILL WARNED ME!

TEELEH IS A MASTER OF DECEPTION. HE IS TRYING TO CONFUSE YOU, THOMAS. COME ON!

WHERE ARE WE GOING?

THE GATHERING. IT'S TIME FOR YOU TO MEET ELYON.

BRMMMMMMMM

BRMMMMMMMMMM

WHAT IS THAT SOUND?

BRMMMMMMMMMM

THOMAS!

WHACK!

RGHHHHHH!

TCHMMMM!

CARLOS!

THOK!

MY GUN...

PHEWT!

PHEWT!

THOMAS!

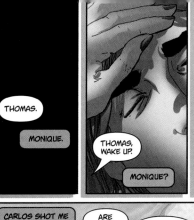

TELL ME ABOUT YOUR DREAMS. HOW REAL ARE THEY?

REAL ENOUGH. BUT THEY ARE THE HISTORIES. A TOTALLY DIFFERENT REALITY.

SO IT'S LIKE YOU'RE REALLY LIVING THERE?

YES.

AND WHAT DO YOU THINK OF THIS PLACE IN YOUR DREAMS?

I WISH SHE HADN'T ASKED THAT...

ACTUALLY, WHEN I'M DREAMING, IT'S LIKE I'M THERE, NOT HERE.

SO I'M LIKE A DREAM?

YOU'RE NOT A DREAM. YOU'RE WALKING RIGHT BESIDE ME, AND I HAVE CHOSEN YOU.

I'M NOT SURE I LIKE THESE DREAMS OF YOURS.

I'M NOT SURE I DO EITHER.

BUT I'M HAVING THEM, I'M LIVING JUST BEFORE THE GREAT DECEPTION, TRYING TO STOP THE RAISON STRAIN.

IT'S SO REAL!

JUST BEFORE YOU WOKE ME, I WAS FIGHTING A MAN WITH A GUN.

A GUN? A WEAPON, I ASSUME. AND WHAT WERE YOU FIGHTING ABOUT?

HE WAS TRYING TO CAPTURE MONIQUE.

MONIQUE?

SHE MEANS NOTHING TO ME!

NOT IN A ROMANTIC WAY.

BUT YOU HAVE TO UNDERSTAND-- SHE'S IMPORTANT! SHE MAY BE THE KEY TO STOPPING THE RAISON STRAIN.

I'M HELPING HER BECAUSE SHE MAY HELP ME SAVE THE WORLD, NOT JUST BECAUSE SHE'S BEAUTIFUL!

UH-OH. THAT WASN'T SMART OF ME.

NOW I'M SURE I DON'T LIKE THESE DREAMS OF YOURS, THOMAS HUNTER.

FROM NOW ON WHEN YO DREAM, DREAM O ME.

NOW COME ON.

MY FIRST GATHERING, AT LEAST THAT I CAN REMEMBER

THE WATERFALL IS POUNDING EVER MORE INTENSELY NOW, THE MIST IS FILLING THE AIR...

...WITH...

...ELYON.

BRMMMMMMMMMMMMM

THIS TREE GROWS AS HIGH AS THE CLIFF.

WHO HAS MADE THIS?

ELYON! ELYON IS OUR CREATOR!

THOMAS!

RACHELLE?

THE BOY. THE GATHERING.

BUT IF I'VE BEEN SLEEPING, THEN...

THOMAS, WAKE UP.

GASP!

KARA!

THOMAS, ARE YOU ALL RIGHT? YOU'VE BEEN SHOT!

TALK TO ME!

ARE YOU HURT?

I DON'T THINK SO... SOMEONE BROKE IN. WE FOUGHT, AND THEN...

AND THEN HE MUST HAVE TAKEN MONIQUE.

AND THEN...

SO WHAT, YOU WERE HEALED IN YOUR DREAM?

YES, BUT... OH, NO.

LISTEN. I THINK I MAY HAVE GIVEN INSTRUCTIONS FOR HOW TO MAKE THE VIRUS TO...

I'M THE UNSUSPECTING FOOL!

WHAT?

TEELEH TRICKED ME INTO REPEATING THE INSTRUCTIONS AND CARLOS MUST HAVE HEARD ME SAY THE WORDS IN MY SLEEP.

CARLOS?

WE HAVE TO GET MONIQUE BACK. SHE'S THE KEY TO THE ANTIVIRUS.

I DON'T UNDERSTAND. WHY DOES CARLOS CARE ABOUT THE ANTIVIRUS?

THINK ABOUT IT. YOU PUT THE VIRUS IN THE AIR, AND THREE WEEKS LATER, EVERYONE'S DEAD, INCLUDING THE PERSON WHO RELEASED IT. BUT IF YOU HAVE THE CURE...

...YOU CAN CONTROL IT. LIKE HAVING THE ONLY NUCLEAR ARSENAL IN THE WORLD.

I ARRANGED TO MEET MONIQUE'S FATHER. I'M PRETTY SURE HE DOESN'T BUY ANY OF THIS. HE JUST WANTS HIS DAUGHTER BACK.

HE'S NOT GOING TO BE HAPPY TO HEAR SHE'S BEEN KIDNAPPED AGAIN...

JACQUES DE RAISON.

YOU *WHAT?*

I DIDN'T LOSE HER.

SHE WAS TAKEN FROM ME.

LET ME EXPLAIN.

YOU HAVE 5 MINUTES. THEN I CALL THE AUTHORITIES.

...AND YOUR DAUGHTER AND I WERE ATTACKED. I WAS SHOT AND LEFT FOR DEAD. MONIQUE WAS TAKEN BY FORCE.

YOU DON'T LOOK LIKE SOMEONE LEFT FOR DEAD.

I CLEAN UP GOOD.

THIS SOUNDS LIKE UTTER NONSENSE.

PLEASE MR. RAISON. THIS GOES WAY BEYOND THOMAS OR MONIQUE.

YES, YES. THE RAISON VACCINE WILL MUTATE AND KILL UNTOLD MILLIONS. YOU'VE TOLD ME.

NOT MILLIONS. BILLIONS.

MONIQUE SUBMITTED THE VACCINE TO A VERY STRINGENT SERIES OF TESTS, I ASSURE YOU.

BUT NOT TO *HIGH HEAT!* SHE TOLD ME HERSELF.

YOU CAN'T SUBSTANTIATE ANY OF THIS.

YOU KIDNAPPED MY DAUGHTER AND YOU EXPECT ME TO BELIEVE IT WAS FOR HER OWN GOOD.

SHE IS MY ONLY DAUGHTER.

DO YOU UNDERSTAND THAT?

YES. AND WE'LL GET HER BACK. HOW LONG WILL IT TAKE TO TEST THE VACCINE?

A DAY OR SO.

THAT'S TOO LON...

MR. RAISON, YOU HAVE A PERSONAL CALL ON LINE 2.

WE'LL STEP OUT.

DON'T YOU DARE TOUCH HER!

MR. RAISON?

THAT WAS THEM, WASN'T IT?

YES. THEY'VE GIVEN ME 72 HOURS TO TURN OVER ALL OUR RESEARCH AND ALL EXISTING SAMPLES OF THE VACCINE. OR THEY KILL HER

IF THEY WERE TO FOLLOW EXACT INSTRUCTIONS, HOW LONG BEFORE THEY COULD HAVE THE VIRUS?

A FEW HOURS, I GUESS.

THEN IT'S ONLY A MATTER OF TIME BEFORE THEY HAVE THE RAISON STRAIN...

THERE IS NO RAISON STRAIN!

YOUR DAUGHTER WILL TELL YOU DIFFERENTLY. BY THEN IT WILL BE TOO LATE.

THEN I'LL GIVE THEM WHAT THEY WANT AND KEEP WHAT I NEED TO REPRODUCE THE VACCINE.

I SUGGEST THAT WE GIVE THEM NOTHING.

TRUST YOU!
HOW DO I KNOW
YOU'RE NOT INVOLVED?
THIS IS CRAZY.

YES, IT IS.
BUT RIGHT NOW, I'M
YOUR ONLY CHANCE
TO GET MONIQUE
BACK.

RUN THOSE HEAT
TESTS, IF A VIRUS
EVOLVES THEN YOU'LL
KNOW I'M TELLING
THE TRUTH.

IN THE
MEANTIME, I'LL
WORK ON FINDING
YOUR DAUGHTER.

SIGH

I'LL NEED YOU
TO MAKE SELECTIVE
CONTACT WITH A FEW
WORLD LEADERS.

I'M NOT
SURE WHAT
YOU'RE
ASKING.

NO ONE
BELIEVES
ME.

HELP ME GET
THE WORD OUT ABOUT
THE DANGER OF THE
RAISON STRAIN TO THE
OUTSIDE WORLD.

IT WILL
GIVE THEM REASON
TO THROW SOME
RESOURCES BEHIND
FINDING MONIQUE.

NOTHING
LIKE A LETHAL
AIRBORNE
VIRUS TO
MOTIVATE
FOLKS.

YOU CAN'T JUST
PLACE CALLS TO WORLD
GOVERNMENTS AND
EXPECT THEM TO BE
ANSWERED.

THEN USE YOUR
PERSONAL CONTACTS.
THE US STATE DEPARTMENT,
THE FRENCH, BRITISH, MAYBE
INDONESIA. WARN THEM OF
THE RISK TO THEIR OWN
NATIONAL SECURITY.

IT WILL BE THE
END OF RAISON
PHARMA...

I REALLY
DON'T THINK YOU
HAVE A CHOICE.

CALL THE LAB. TELL
THEM THEY HAVE 6
HOURS TO RUN THE
HEAT TESTS.

I'LL GO
LOOK FOR
MONIQUE.

GO?
WHERE?

DREAMLAND.

IT'S TIME TO WAKE UP SLEEPY HEAD.

HI.

COME ON, IT'S A BEAUTIFUL DAY. LET'S GO FOR A WALK!

EVERY TIME I WAKE UP I HAVE TO MAKE THE TRANSITION. THE SWITCH.

IT'S GETTING EASIER

THOMAS, WOULD YOU LIKE TO KISS ME?

KISS?

YOU DON'T WANT TO?

NO, I MEAN YES. YES. OF COURSE I DO!

YOU JUST CAUGHT ME OFF GUARD, THAT'S ALL.

A KISS MIGHT HELP YOU TO REMEMBER...

YOU DO REMEMBER HOW TO KISS DON'T YOU?

I'D BE HAPPY TO SHOW YOU EXACTLY HOW IT'S DONE.

NOW, TELL ME THAT WASN'T REAL!

MAYBE SPARK YOUR MEMORY...

I HOPE SO.

I WISH YOU DIDN'T HAVE THOSE DREAMS, OF THE OTHER PLACE.

YOU'RE NOT THE ONLY ONE.

THERE'S SOMETHING YOU CAN DO, YOU KNOW... TO SLEEP WITHOUT DREAMING.

YES... A FRUIT...

IT IS CALLED THE RAMBUTAN.

THEN I WOULD NEVER LEAVE THIS PLACE...

...NEVER LEAVE YOU.

YOUR DREAMS OF THE HISTORIES WOULD BE GONE.

JUST LIKE THAT.

JUST LIKE THAT.

SO, THOMAS HUNTER, BACK TO THE GREAT ROMANCE!

WHEN ARE YOU GOING TO RESCUE ME?

IS IT POSSIBLE THAT RACHELLE IS SOMEHOW CONNECTED TO MONIQUE?

PERHAPS THE CONNECTION BETWEEN THE TWO WORLDS GOES BEYOND JUST ME...

MAYBE WHAT HAPPENS IN BANGKOK DEPENDS ON WHAT HAPPENS HERE?

AND VISA VERSA...

THOMAS!

THOMAS HUNTER, THERE YOU ARE!

I HAVE BEEN LOOKING FOR YOU!

WHAT IS THAT YOU'RE HOLDING?

IT'S SOMETHING I REMEMBERED FROM THE HISTORIES.

IT'S A WEAPON!

TO SCARE THE VERMIN!

IT DOESN'T LOOK PARTICULARLY SCARY.

AHH, MAYBE NOT TO YOU. BUT THE SHATAIKI ARE TERRIFIED OF THE COLORED FOREST.

THIS WEAPON IS FASHIONED FROM COLORED WOOD. SO, IT FOLLOWS THAT THEY WOULD BE TERRIFIED OF IT AS WELL.

WE COULD USE THESE WEAPONS ON OUR EXPEDITIONS!

THIS IS CALLED A SWORD.

BUT YOU'VE FORGOTTEN TO GIVE IT A SHARP EDGE.

SHOW ME.

WELL IT NEEDS TO BE FLAT HERE AND SHARP ALONG SO THIS EDGE SO IT CAN CUT.

MAY I?

THERE!

THOMAS, WAKE UP!

SORRY, YOU SAID FIVE HOURS BUT I FELL ASLEEP.

IT'S BEEN EIGHT.

WHAT TIME IS IT?

CLOSE TO NOON.

UNGHHH. I'M EXHAUSTED.

YOU FOUND SOMETHING OUT, DIDN'T YOU?

WHAT?

I THINK I CAN TURN OFF MY DREAMS.

COMPLETELY.

WHAT GOOD WOULD THAT DO? WHO WOULD RESCUE US THEN?

RESCUE?

COME ON!

WHAT IS IT?

A MAP! IS RAISON AWAKE? WE NEED TO WAKE HIM UP!

I NEED A MAP KARA!

A GREAT WHITE CAVE OF BOTTLES A DAY'S WALK TO THE EAST... WHERE A RIVER AND THE FOREST MEET.

WHERE IS THAT?

WHAT?

THAT'S WHERE SHE IS. WE HAVE TO FIGURE OUT WHAT THAT MEANS.

THAT'S YOUR...THAT'S ALL YOU KNOW?

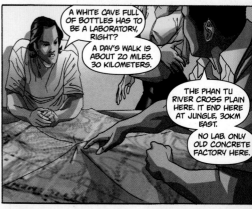

A WHITE CAVE FULL OF BOTTLES HAS TO BE A LABORATORY, RIGHT?

A DAY'S WALK IS ABOUT 20 MILES. 30 KILOMETERS.

THE PHAN TU RIVER CROSS PLAIN HERE. IT END HERE AT JUNGLE, 30KM EAST.

NO LAB. ONLY OLD CONCRETE FACTORY HERE.

A CONCRETE PLANT? RIGHT THERE?

YES, BUT NO LONGER IN USE.

HOW DO YOU KNOW THIS INFORMATION IS ACCURATE...

WE NEED THE HELICOPTER, MR. RAISON. IS YOUR PILOT HERE?

YES BUT, YOU'RE UNDER HOUSE ARREST! THIS IS NOT POSSIBLE!

NONE OF THIS IS POSSIBLE, MR. RAISON. NONE OF THIS.

BUT IF ANYONE CAN RESCUE HER I CAN.

OPEN IT.

WARNING
AREA

SO MONIQUE, ARE YOU READY TO WRITE HISTORY?

YOU RECOGNIZE ME, DON'T YOU? WE'VE MET BEFORE...AT A SYMPOSIUM, YEARS AGO.

WHICH IS A PROBLEM.

REMOVE IT, CARLOS.

VALBORG SVENSSON. YOU WILL SPEND THE REST OF YOUR LIFE IN A PRISON FAR WORSE THAN THIS ONE.

HIGHLY UNLIKELY. TELL ME, DO YOU KNOW WHAT HAPPENS TO THE RAISON VACCINE WHEN IT'S HEATED TO 179.47 DEGREES AND HELD THERE FOR TWO HOURS? WE DO.

YOU CAN THANK YOUR FRIEND THOMAS FOR THAT... TOO BAD HE'S DEAD.

YOU'LL BE WORKING FOR US FOR A WHILE MS. RAISON. JACQUES IS SENDING EVERYTHING YOU'LL NEED.

AND MONIQUE, NOBODY'S COMING FOR YOU.

AND JUST IN CASE YOU WERE CONSIDERING GOING SOMEWHERE WITHOUT ME,

THAT RATHER LARGE PILL CARLOS FORCED YOU TO SWALLOW...

...WAS A RADIO-CONTROLLED DETONATOR.

STRAY MORE THAN 50 METERS AND, WELL...

...I'LL LEAVE THAT TO YOUR IMAGINATION.

THERE!

NO ONE GO HERE FOR LONG TIME.

WE STILL NEED TO BE VERY CAREFUL.

YOU GET BEHIND THE SHED. COVER ME WITH YOUR GUN.

YOU KNOW HOW TO SHOOT, RIGHT?

OF COURSE.

GOOD. COVER ME, AND AS SOON AS I CLEAR THE ENTRY, FOLLOW ME IN.

YOU GO, I FOLLOW.

READY?

THOMAS!

MONIQUE!

YOU...YOU'RE DEAD. I SAW HIM SHOOT YOU.

YOU'RE HERE!

RACHELLE TOLD ME YOU'D BE HERE... IN THE WHITE CAVE WITH BOTTLES.

I CAN'T BELIEVE I FOUND YOU! INCREDIBLE.

THANK GOD YOU'RE SAFE.

THOMAS...

WE HAVE TO GET OUT OF HERE, FAST.

THOMAS. WE HAVE A PROBLEM.

LET'S TALK ABOUT IT LATER. COME ON!

I CAN'T!

HE FORCED ME TO SWALLOW AN EXPLOSIVE DEVICE.

IF I GO MORE THAN FIFTY METERS FROM HIM, IT WILL KILL ME!

I CAN'T LEAVE!

MUTA..

THWACKK!

BANG!

UNGHH

IMPOSSIBLE!

YOU GAVE THEM THE VACCINE?

THEY GAVE ME ONE HOUR, MR. HUNTER. MY DAUGHTER'S LIFE WAS ON THE LINE.

...IT'S NOT JUST YOUR DAUGHTER'S LIFE THAT'S ON THE LINE HERE JACQUES!

FOR ME IT IS.

SHE GAVE ME THIS TO PERSUADE YOU TO LISTEN TO ME.

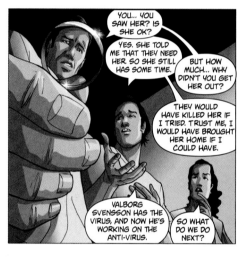

YOU... YOU SAW HER? IS SHE OK?

YES. SHE TOLD ME THAT THEY NEED HER, SO SHE STILL HAS SOME TIME.

BUT HOW MUCH... WHY DIDN'T YOU GET HER OUT?

THEY WOULD HAVE KILLED HER IF I TRIED. TRUST ME, I WOULD HAVE BROUGHT HER HOME IF I COULD HAVE.

VALBORG SVENSSON HAS THE VIRUS, AND NOW HE'S WORKING ON THE ANTI-VIRUS.

SO WHAT DO WE DO NEXT?

I NEED THOSE HEAT TESTS COMPLETED TONIGHT.

TRY HEATING THE VACCINE TO EXACTLY 179.47 DEGREES AND MAINTAIN THE HEAT FOR TWO HOURS.

DID YOU CATCH THAT? GOOD. WATCH FOR MUTATIONS AND GET BACK TO ME IMMEDIATELY.

I STILL HOPE YOU'RE WRONG MR. HUNTER.

I KNOW VALBORG SVENSSON.

AND?

IF YOU'RE RIGHT? GOD HELP US.

ARE YOU OKAY THOMAS? THERE'S BLOOD ON YOUR T-SHIRT.

CARLOS SHOT ME. AGAIN.

BUT I FLIPPED BACK FROM THE GREEN FOREST TO HERE, AND THEN I WAS FINE.

THE MIST FROM ELYON'S WATERFALL HEALED ME...

KARA, WE HAVE TO FIND THAT ANTIVIRUS, OTHERWISE THIS IS GOING TO BE A LONELY PLANET.

BUT AT LEAST JACQUES IS STARTING TO BELIEVE YOU. HIS LAB CAN HELP.

I DON'T THINK THEY CAN FIND IT WITHOUT MONIQUE.

THEN YOU NEED TO GO BACK THERE. YOU NEED TO DREAM.

I'M PRETTY WIRED RIGHT NOW, I DON'T KNOW IF I CAN.

THERE'S NO OTHER WAY. YOU HAVE TO DO WHATEVER IT TAKES TO GET MORE INFORMATION ON THE RAISON STRAIN AND THE ANTIVIRUS.

THE BLACK FOREST.

HERE, THESE WILL HELP.

OK, KNOCK ME OUT.

UNNGHH

I'M BACK. AGAIN.

DESTINATION: THE BLACK FOREST.

BUT HOW CAN I GET TEELEH TO GIVE ME WHAT I WANT?

TANIS' SWORD.

IT'S POISON TO TEELEH.

GOOD MORNING, MY DREAMER.

FINDING MONIQUE AGAIN IS GOING TO BE HARDER.

TIME.

IT'S RUNNING OUT.

THE SWORD.

I NEED TO FIND IT.

SOMEWHERE AROUND HERE...

THERE!

FWOOM

ARE YOU READY TEELEH?

THIS IS IT.

CAN I DO THIS?

TAKE ON A THOUSAND OF THEM WITH ONE SWORD?

TEELEH WANTS TANIS. I CAN USE THAT.

WHAT'S THIS?

A SHARP STICK... ANOTHER WEAPON MAYBE?

GOOD TO HAVE AN EXTRA CARD TO PLAY.

SOMETHING UP MY SLEEVE.

THERE THEY ARE.

WHERE'S TEELEH?

THEY'RE PRETTY QUIET AND THEY'RE NOT MOVING.

STRANGE.

TEELEH!

COME OUT AND FACE ME!

SO, YOU THINK YOU HAVE POWER OVER ME?

I NEED TO KNOW MORE ABOUT THE HISTORIES.

I SEE. AND ARE YOU STILL INTERESTED IN YOUR SHIP?

SHIP...?

BILL!

IT IS REAL!

I'M GONNA NEED BILL TO FLY THIS THING OUT OF HERE.

HUH?

HOW CAN YOU TOUCH THAT SWORD?

TANIS SAID THE WOOD WAS POISON TO HIM!

BUT – IT'S NOT RED ANYMORE!

THE SHIP! IT'S GONE!

THERE WAS NO SHIP!

HE IS THE DECEIVER...

SHRIEK!

ARGHHHH!

UNNGGHH

YOU THINK YOU CAN JUST SLEEP THROUGH THIS HUMAN?

WAKE UP!

WELCOME TO THE LAND OF THE LIVING.

OR SHOULD I SAY, THE LAND OF THE DEAD.

WE MAKE NO REAL DISTINCTION HERE.

MASTER... WE HAVE HIM.

BRING. HIM.

THOMAS, I'VE PREPARED A SPECIAL TREAT FOR YOU. I THINK YOU WILL LIKE IT.

BEAUTIFUL ISN'T IT? HE'S BEEN WAITING FOR YOU THOMAS.

YOU DO REMEMBER HIM, DON'T YOU?

BILL.

AND YOU THOUGHT YOU COULD DEFEAT ME WITH ONE MEASLY SWORD.

YOU ARE IN DEEP THOMAS HUNTER, THERE'S ONLY ONE WAY OUT FOR YOU NOW.

KILL BILL. TAKE THIS SWORD AND KILL HIM AND I WILL RELEASE YOU.

OTHERWISE, YOU'LL BOTH HANG HERE FOR A VERY LONG TIME.

PAINFULLY LONG.

WHO WOULD EVER HAVE GUESSED?

HISTORY CHANGED BECAUSE OF A FEW DROPS OF AN INNOCUOUS-LOOKING YELLOW LIQUID...

...AND ONE MAN WHO HAD THE STOMACH TO USE IT.

BRING HER UP.

MS. DE RAISON.

SIT.

YOU THINK MY FATHER ISN'T ALREADY WORKING ON AN ANTIVIRUS?

AND HOW LONG WILL IT TAKE HIM? MONTHS AT BEST.

AND HE DOESN'T KNOW ABOUT YOUR BACK DOOR, DOES HE?

WHAT! HOW DO YOU...

SO, IT'S TRUE. OUR SOURCE SAID THAT YOU OFTEN CONSTRUCT A BACK DOOR, INTERESTING.

WHAT DO YOU SAY MS. DE RAISON?

NO.

NO?

NO.

I'LL GIVE MS DE RAISON 12 HOURS TO CHANGE HER MIND, BEFORE WE CHANGE IT FOR HER.

EVERYTHING IS READY, CARLOS?

YES.

THEN I WILL HANDLE THE NEXT MOVE. CAN YOU HANDLE THE AMERICAN?

YOU HAVE ALREADY FAILED TWICE.

HE HAS PROVEN TO BE... A CHALLENGE.

WE HAVE INFORMATION THAT HE HAS FOUND A NEW HOTEL. MAKE NO MISTAKE THIS TIME CARLOS.

WE RELEASE THE VIRUS THROUGHOUT THE WORLD WITHIN TWENTY-FOUR HOURS.

THEN WE CONTACT THE WORLD'S LEADERS AND MAKE OUR DEMANDS, CLAIMING WE HAVE THE ANTI-VIRUS.

IF MONIQUE CAN'T HELP US CREATE THE ANTI-VIRUS, THEN WE'LL BE DEAD...

"...JUST LIKE EVERYBODY ELSE."

TANIS!

WHERE IS HE?

THOMAS! OH MY GOODNESS, THOMAS!

MICHAL? WHAT'S WRONG?

IT'S TANIS. HE IS HEADED FOR THE BLACK FOREST.

WHAT! ARE YOU SURE? AFTER WHAT HAPPENED YESTERDAY, I WAS SURE—

HE WAS HEADED STRAIGHT FOR IT WHEN I LEFT TO FIND YOU. HE WAS RUNNING.

WHY DIDN'T YOU STOP HIM?

IT'S NOT MY PLACE!

IT'S GOOD TO SEE YOU AGAIN MY FRIEND. I'M GLAD YOU RETURNED.

YOU'RE DIFFERENT THAN WHAT I EXPECTED.

HOW SO?

I HEARD YOU WERE QUITE CLEVER.

BUT YOU PRETEND YOU'RE DIFFERENT THAN YOU REALLY ARE, WHEN YOU KNOW YOU WILL BE FOUND OUT.

YOU LIKE THAT, DON'T YOU?

YOU LIKE BEING CLEVER. IT'S WHY YOU'VE COME HERE.

YOU WANT TO LEARN MORE.

MORE KNOWLEDGE.

THE... TRUTH.

THEN... SHOW ME THE TRUTH.

I INTEND TO...

IS THAT BETTER?

NO, IT'S MUCH WORSE.

YOU'RE THE MOST HIDEOUS CREATURE I COULD EVER HAVE IMAGINED.

BUT I POSSESS THE TRUTH. WOULD YOU LIKE TO HEAR?

COME CLOSER. YOU'RE SAFE WITH THE WOOD IN YOUR HAND.

YOU WANT TO KNOW MORE ABOUT ME SO YOU CAN DESTROY ME.

HOW...?

BECAUSE I KNOW FAR MORE THAN YOU DO, MY FRIEND. COME CLOSER.

AAAAAAAA!

TO BE CONTINUED

RED

THE HEROIC RESCUE

HOW DID THEY GET SO CLOSE WITHOUT US KNOWING?

THE MAIN BODY IS MOVING SOUTH, ALONG THE CLIFFS.

THEY'RE TRYING TO ENGAGE US IN THE NATALGA GAP. THE MAIN FORCE WILL FLANK US.

AND THEY LOOK TO SUCCEED.

ONLY IF WE LET THEM, WILLIAM.

THEY HAVE NUMBERS ON THEIR SIDE, BUT ELYON IS ON OURS. AND THAT IS ENOUGH.

THEY ARE A CURSED PEOPLE, DISEASED AND ROTTING.

SCABS.

HE HASN'T HEARD ABOUT THE ANTIVIRUS WE HAVE. SO HE THINKS IT'S SAFE TO KILL ME. I THOUGHT IT WOULD SOUND MORE CONVINCING COMING FROM YOU.

ANTI---? THOMAS YOU'RE BLEEDING...

I ONLY HAVE TO BUY HER A COUPLE SECONDS.

KARA, LISTEN TO ME.

UNDER THE BED.

YOU WON'T HAVE MUCH TIME.

GO!

SCHTT

THWACK!

THOMAS, WAKE UP. ARE YOU OK? GAINS JUST CALLED. I TOLD HIM ABOUT CARLOS. HE WANTS TO SEE US.

YEAH, I'M OK. LET'S GO. HE NEEDS MY HELP, AND I NEED HIS.

IF GAINS IS LOOKING FOR US, THEY MUST HAVE MORE NEWS OF THE VIRUS.

LET'S HOPE SO.

MR. GAINS WILL BE WITH YOU SHORTLY.

CARLOS WILL BE BACK...

GAINS WAS RIGHT ABOUT GETTING MORE SECURITY FOR MY SUITE.

BUT WHAT I DON'T UNDERSTAND IS... THIRTEEN YEARS?

SOMETHING LIKE THAT.

YOU'VE BEEN IN THE OTHER WORLD FOR THAT LONG? YOU'RE SURE?

QUITE SURE.

HOW IS THAT POSSIBLE? YOU'RE NOT THIRTEEN YEARS OLDER, ARE YOU?

MY BODY ISN'T, NAY—

NAY?

SORRY.

NAY... SOUNDS OLD.

MR. GAINS.

GOOD. WE'RE GOING TO NEED THESE DREAMS OF YOURS.

NEVER IMAGINED I WOULD EVER SAY SOMETHING LIKE THAT, BUT THEN AGAIN, I NEVER IMAGINED WE WOULD FACE SUCH A MONSTROUS EVIL.

CAN I GET EITHER OF YOU A DRINK?

NO THANKS.

I HATE TO ADMIT IT BUT WE'VE UNDERESTIMATED YOU FROM THE BEGINNING, THOMAS.

I CAN ASSURE YOU—THAT HAS JUST CHANGED.

I'LL CUT TO THE CHASE. LAST NIGHT AT BANGKOK INTERNATIONAL A MAN WAS REPORTED HARASSING SEVERAL FLIGHT ATTENDANTS, BEING UNUSUALLY FRIENDLY-SHAKING HANDS AND HUGGING STRANGERS AND SO ON—ALL OVER THE AIRPORT.

WE FOUND HIS BELONGINGS AND A BRIEFCASE IN ONE OF THE AIRPORT TOILETS. LAST NIGHT WE CONCLUDED AN ANALYSIS OF THAT BRIEFCASE.

ANY GUESS AS TO WHAT THEY FOUND?

THE RAISON STRAIN.

I'M NOT SURE YOU REALIZE THE FULL EXTENT OF WHAT I'M FACING IN THE OTHER WORLD, MERTON. I NEED HELP.

THEN LET ME HELP YOU.

I'M LEADING WHAT REMAINS OF MY ARMY, THE FOREST GUARD, AGAINST AN INCREDIBLY UNEQUAL BATTLE WITH THE HORDE.

IF I DON'T FIND A WAY TO BRING DOWN A CLIFF ON TOP OF THEM, OUR ARMY, AND THE WOMEN AND CHILDREN IN THE NEARBY FOREST, WILL ALL BE SLAUGHTERED.

THAT MAY SEEM LIKE A LOT OF HOGWASH TO YOU, BUT IF I DIE THERE, I DIE HERE.

I'LL DO EVERYTHING I CAN TO HELP YOU, IF YOU'LL HELP ME STAY ALIVE.

I WILL, THOMAS. FOR THE SAKE OF YOUR CREDIBILITY, I SUGGEST THAT WE DON'T SHARE ALL THESE DETAILS WITH THE FOLKS IN WASHINGTON.

UNDERSTOOD.

WE'RE IN A CANYON LAND. ROCK RICH IN COPPER, TIN ORES. I NEED TO FIND A WAY TO MAKE AN EXPLOSIVE.

BLACK POWDER

NOT DYNAMITE?

BLACK POWDER WAS FIRST MADE BY COMBINING COMMON ELEMENTS.

I'LL GET THE C.I.A. TO SEND YOU A HOW-TO AND YOU CAN REVIEW ON THE WAY TO D.C.

LATER

GAINS WAS RIGHT. TAKE A LOOK AT THE THREE INGREDIENTS. THERE ARE SOME SUBSTITUTES TOO; YOU COULD USE THE SUGAR FOR THE CHARCOAL.

I HAVE TO MEMORIZE THIS, AND THE RATIOS.

LET'S JUST HOPE I CAN FIND WHAT I NEED.

ELYON'S STRENGTH.

ELYON'S STRENGTH.

THIS IS THE MOST ABSURD THING I'VE EVER HEARD!

WE'RE ALMOST OUT OF TIME. IF WE LOSE HERE, THE ENTIRE FOREST WILL FALL. ALL I'M ASKING FOR IS YOUR TRUST AND A LITTLE HOPE.

CHARCOAL WE HAVE, RIGHT? WE BURN IT. A FEW FAST RIDERS CAN RETRIEVE AN AMPLE SUPPLY AND HAVE IT HERE BY MIDNIGHT.

SULFUR IS FOUND IN CAVES LIKE THE ONES AT THE NORTH END OF THE GAP. SEND SOME MEN.

WHAT ABOUT THE SALT?

SALTPETER IT'S A WHITE, TRANSLUCENT MINERAL.

AND WHERE DO WE FIND THIS?

IN THE CAVES.

WE'LL NEED TO BREAK OFF THE CONES, HEAT THEM IN A LARGE FIRE, AND PRAY THAT SULFUR FLOWS FROM THE PORES.

SIR! WILLIAM THINKS HE MAY HAVE FOUND THE MINERAL YOU SEEK!

NOW WHAT?

NOW WE GRIND THEM TO A FINE POWDER, CAREFULLY MIX THEM, PACK THEM INTO SMALL SACKS, AND PRAY TO ELYON THAT THERE'S ENOUGH FORCE TO DO SOME DAMAGE.

WILL IT WORK?

WE WILL KNOW SOON ENOUGH.

ELYON!

ELYON!

ELYON!

HUNTER!

HUNTER!   HUNTER!

SO TIRED. WE NEED TO BATHE, AND REST.

I NEED TO DREAM.

CIPHUS, IT'S THE SOUTHERN FOREST.

WE MAY LOSE IT.

JAMOUS NEEDS HELP. BUT IF THE GUARD VACATES THIS FOREST WHILE SO MANY ARE COMING FOR THE ANNUAL GATHERING—

WELL, WE WON'T CANCEL THE GATHERING. AS HIGH PRIEST I CAN PROMISE YOU THAT.

WE COULD USE THE BOMBS!

THE BOMBS?

FROM THOMAS'S DREAMS IN BANGKOK.

THE BLACK POWDER WON'T DO ANYTHING IN THE OPEN DESERT.

WE CAN SEND THREE HUNDRED MEN, NO MORE.

WHAT IS BANGKOK?

THE WORLD IN HIS DREAMS. WHEN HE DREAMS, HE BELIEVES HE GOES TO ANOTHER PLACE, THAT HE'S ACTUALLY LIVING IN THE ANCIENT HISTORIES.

HE THINKS HE CAN STOP THE VIRUS THAT LED TO THE GREAT DECEPTION IN HIS DREAM WORLD.

THIS IS WHY YOU ARE SO INTERESTED IN THE BOOK OF HISTORIES? TO SAVE A DREAM WORLD?

THE DREAMS HELPED US DEFEAT THE HORDE.

PERHAPS. IF YOU SEEK TO KNOW ABOUT THE BOOKS, ASK JEREMIAH OF SOUTHERN. HE IS WISE.

JEREMIAH OF SOUTHERN, THE MAN WHO HAD ONCE BEEN A SCAB?

THERE IS ANOTHER MATTER MORE PRESSING THAN DREAMS, THOMAS.

JUSTIN?

HE IS BETRAYING US ALL WITH HIS TALK. MORE FOLLOW HIM EACH DAY, FURTHERING HIS HERESY.

WHAT DO YOU SUGGEST?

A MEETING OF THE COUNCIL. MANY ARE ALREADY ON THEIR WAY.

THEY SET FIRE TO THE FOREST AFTER THREE DAYS OF BATTLE.

THEY'VE NEVER DONE THAT BEFORE. BUT THEY'VE NEVER BEEN SO CLOSE, EITHER.

THEY'VE NEVER FOUGHT LIKE THIS. MORE ORGANIZED.

FLANKING MANEUVERS THEY'D NEVER USED BEFORE.

THIS IS THE WORK OF MARTYN.

JAMOUS, A RIDER APPROACHES.

MARKUS?

WHAT'S THIS?

I WOKE UP AND MY FINGER WAS CUT. BUT IT HAPPENED IN MY DREAM.

NO, THOMAS. I REMEMBER IT CLEARLY. BEFORE I SAW MONIQUE'S FACE, SHE HANDLED SOME PARCHMENT THAT CUT HER FINGER.

MAYBE YOU IMAGINED YOU WERE CUTTING YOURSELF THERE, WORKING ON THE VIRUS I'VE SPOKEN OF MANY TIMES?

THOMAS, YOU HAVE TO BELIEVE ME! I SAW...THE COMPUTER. OR A...A MICRO... SOMETHING.

THERE WAS A DEVICE THAT LOOKS INTO VERY SMALL THINGS. HOW COULD I KNOW THAT?

WE NEVER SPOKE OF THESE THINGS. YOU NEED TO BELIEVE ME LIKE I BELIEVED YOU.

I DO BELIEVE YOU, BUT...I'M THOMAS IN BOTH REALITIES, AND I LOOK THE SAME IN BOTH. YOU DON'T LOOK LIKE MONIQUE.

DO YOU KNOW, IS MONIQUE SLEEPING NOW?

I DON'T THINK SHE KNOWS ABOUT ME.

PERHAPS BECAUSE SHE HASN'T DREAMED OF YOU!

I HAVE TO GET THE OTHER BOOKS OF HISTORIES BEFORE THE HORDE MOVES!

NO. YOU MUST DREAM.

THERE ISN'T TIME.

BUT, THOMAS...

I THINK I KNOW WHERE MONIQUE IS BEING HELD.

THUD!

THOMAS!

WHAT HAPPENED?

SORRY. I JUST...

WHAT'S THIS? WHAT'S HAPPENING?

NOTHING. IT'S JUST A SCRATCH.

THE NEEDLE.

WE NEED TO GO. THEY'RE CALLING FOR YOU.

THE COUNCIL. JUSTIN IS COMING.

WHO IS?

HALF THE VILLAGE IS THERE TO RECEIVE HIM ALREADY.

TO RECEIVE HIM?

MONIQUE?

NO. NOT MONIQUE.

RACHELLE.

WHO HAD CRIED HERSELF TO SLEEP LAST NIGHT AFTER LEARNING THE TRUTH ABOUT HER BROTHER, JOHAN.

MIKIL! WAKE UP!

THOMAS?

HURRY, WE HAVE BUSINESS!

HAVE THE SCOUTS REPORTED IN?

NO. I'LL TELL YOU ON THE WAY.

WHY ARE WE HEADED TO THE STABLES?

LISTEN TO ME. WHAT WOULD YOU SAY IF I TOLD YOU JUSTIN MIGHT HAVE BETRAYAL IN MIND?

I KNEW IT! HE'LL BE THE END OF THE FOREST! BUT, HOW DO YOU KNOW?

I DREAMED.

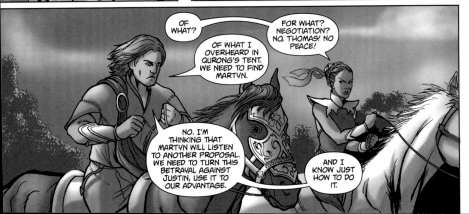

OF WHAT?

FOR WHAT? NEGOTIATION? NO, THOMAS! NO PEACE!

OF WHAT I OVERHEARD IN QURONG'S TENT. WE NEED TO FIND MARTYN.

NO. I'M THINKING THAT MARTYN WILL LISTEN TO ANOTHER PROPOSAL. WE NEED TO TURN THIS BETRAYAL AGAINST JUSTIN, USE IT TO OUR ADVANTAGE.

AND I KNOW JUST HOW TO DO IT.

GENERAL MARTYN'S TENT.

COMING HERE WAS EITHER VERY SMART OR VERY STUPID. WHY HAVE YOU COME?

AM I?

I KNOW YOU'RE CONSPIRING WITH JUSTIN AND QURONG AGAINST THE FOREST PEOPLE.

YOU WILL USE JUSTIN TO OFFER OUR PEOPLE PEACE, THEN BETRAY US.

A SMALL PRICE TO PAY FOR PEACE.

OR CONQUEST.

IT DOESN'T HAVE TO BE THIS WAY, JOHAN. PEACE MAY NOT BE POSSIBLE, BUT A TRUCE IS.

AS JUSTIN PROPOSED. A TRUCE.

THAT WILL END IN RIVERS OF BLOODSHED, MOSTLY YOUR PEOPLE'S. THE ONLY WAY TO A TRUCE IS FOR YOU TO LEAD THE HORDE INSTEAD OF QURONG.

I COULD HAVE YOU KILLED FOR SUCH WORDS. YOU'RE SUGGESTING A REVOLT AGAINST QURONG, MY FATHER.

I KNEW YOUR FATHER, AND QURONG IS NOT HIM.

HE IS. SINCE THE TIME HE WAS CALLED TANIS, HE HAS BEEN A FATHER TO ME.

TANIS? QURONG IS TANIS?!

I WILL ENSURE YOUR SAFE PASSAGE INTO THE FOREST WITH QURONG AND JUSTIN. BRING A THOUSAND OF YOUR BEST WARRIORS IF YOU MUST.

BEFORE THE PEOPLE, YOU WILL EXPOSE THE BETRAYAL OF JUSTIN AND QURONG, AND I WILL SWEAR YOU SAY THE TRUTH. WE WILL CONDEMN QURONG TO DEATH, AND YOU WILL RULE.

YOU THINK I'M FOOLISH ENOUGH TO WALK INTO A TRAP? QURONG WILL NEVER ALLOW ME TO ACCOMPANY HIM. IT IS TOO RISKY.

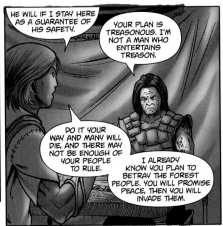

HE WILL IF I STAY HERE AS A GUARANTEE OF HIS SAFETY.

YOUR PLAN IS TREASONOUS. I'M NOT A MAN WHO ENTERTAINS TREASON.

DO IT YOUR WAY AND MANY WILL DIE, AND THERE MAY NOT BE ENOUGH OF YOUR PEOPLE TO RULE.

I ALREADY KNOW YOU PLAN TO BETRAY THE FOREST PEOPLE. YOU WILL PROMISE PEACE, THEN YOU WILL INVADE THEM.

I WILL CONSIDER IT.

:GAAASP:

RACHELLE?

BE QUIET—THEY'RE OUTSIDE.

WE'RE IN THE HORDE CAMP.

YOU WERE DEAD... ELYON'S WATER HEALED YOU.

HIS WATER HEALS AGAIN?

YES. HE HEALED ME TOO.

IT'S HIM, THOMAS.

WHO?

JUSTIN. JUSTIN IS THE BOY. HE'S THE BOY.

WHAT?

DON'T YOU SEE? THE SIGNS WERE ALL THERE, WE JUST DIDN'T SEE THEM. OR DIDN'T WANT TO SEE THEM.

THE PROPHECY...

ONE DAY, WHEN YOU THINK IT CAN'T GET ANY WORSE, THERE WILL BE A WAY.

IN ONE INCREDIBLE BLOW WE WILL DESTROY THE HEART OF EVIL.

MY DEAR, DEAR GOD, ELYON!

WHAT?

I'VE BETRAYED HIM. IT'S A SETUP. ALL OF IT.

WE'VE GOT TO GET OUT OF HERE.

THEY'RE GOING TO KILL HIM.

FOR OVER AN HOUR THE DULL SOUND OF THICK METAL RODS LANDING ON JUSTIN FILLED THE AIR.

HE NEVER CRIED OUT, EVEN WHEN THE SOUND OF SPLINTERING BONE COULD BE HEARD DEEP WITHIN THE CROWD.

STOP! STOP!

STOP THIS!

NO! NO!

WHAT IS THIS? WHO AUTHORIZED THIS?

STAND DOWN, THOMAS, UNLESS YOU WISH TO JOIN HIM.

TWACK!

STOP! YOU DON'T UNDERSTAND!

WE HAVE TO STOP THIS!

WE WILL NOT! THAT WOULD DEFY THE ORDER OF COUNCIL AND ELYON HIMSELF!

THE VERDICT HAS BEEN CAST. THE FATE OF OUR PEOPLE DEPENDS ON THIS EXCHANGE.

ARE YOU SO BLIND? THE PEACE WON'T LAST! YOU THINK YOU CAN TRUST THESE SCABS TO KEEP PEACE? IT'S ALL A LIE!

QURONG IS TANIS! HE'S BLINDED BY TEELEH, AND HE'S FOUND A WAY TO KILL ELYON!

ELYON WOULD NEVER LET A SCAB ABUSE HIM, ANY MORE THAN HE WOULD LET TEELEH ABUSE HIM.

IF HE IS ELYON, THEN LET HIM SAVE HIMSELF. HE IS A MAN, THOMAS. A *MAN*.

THE TIME HAS COME.

TO THE TOWER.

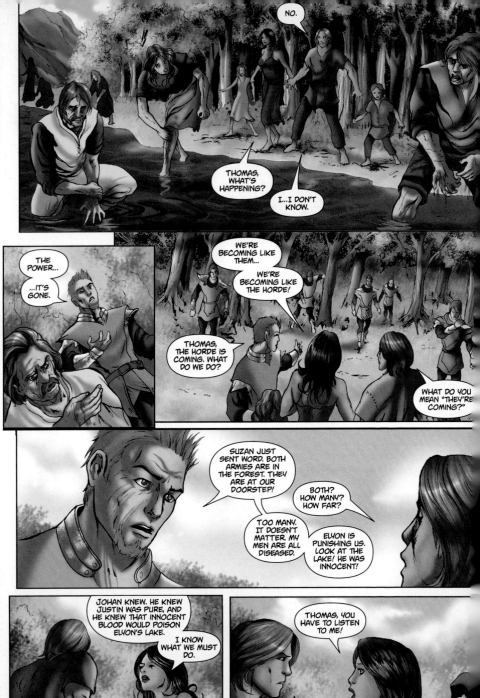

NO.

THOMAS, WHAT'S HAPPENING?

I...I DON'T KNOW.

THE POWER...

...IT'S GONE.

WE'RE BECOMING LIKE THEM...

WE'RE BECOMING LIKE THE HORDE!

THOMAS, THE HORDE IS COMING. WHAT DO WE DO?

WHAT DO YOU MEAN "THEY'RE COMING?"

SUZAN JUST SENT WORD. BOTH ARMIES ARE IN THE FOREST. THEY ARE AT OUR DOORSTEP!

BOTH? HOW MANY? HOW FAR?

TOO MANY. IT DOESN'T MATTER. MY MEN ARE ALL DISEASED.

ELYON IS PUNISHING US. LOOK AT THE LAKE! HE WAS INNOCENT!

JOHAN KNEW. HE KNEW JUSTIN WAS PURE, AND HE KNEW THAT INNOCENT BLOOD WOULD POISON ELYON'S LAKE.

I KNOW WHAT WE MUST DO.

JUSTIN TOLD ME TO DIE WITH HIM. DROWN WITH HIM, THOMAS, LIKE WE DID YEARS AGO.

THOMAS, YOU HAVE TO LISTEN TO ME!

YOU'RE SUGGESTING WE RUN INTO THIS LAKE AND DROWN OURSELVES? KILL OURSELVES?!

YOU WOULD RATHER LIVE LIKE THIS?

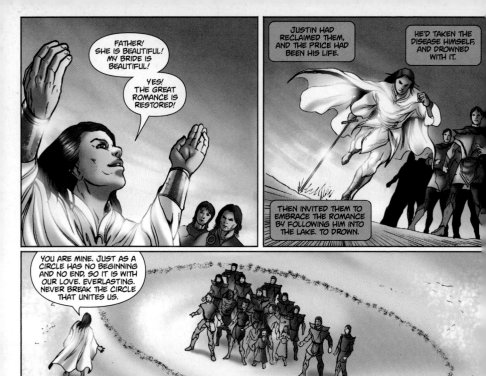

FATHER! SHE IS BEAUTIFUL! MY BRIDE IS BEAUTIFUL!

YES! THE GREAT ROMANCE IS RESTORED!

JUSTIN HAD RECLAIMED THEM, AND THE PRICE HAD BEEN HIS LIFE.

HE'D TAKEN THE DISEASE HIMSELF, AND DROWNED WITH IT.

THEN INVITED THEM TO EMBRACE THE ROMANCE BY FOLLOWING HIM INTO THE LAKE. TO DROWN.

YOU ARE MINE. JUST AS A CIRCLE HAS NO BEGINNING AND NO END, SO IT IS WITH OUR LOVE. EVERLASTING. NEVER BREAK THE CIRCLE THAT UNITES US.

THIS WAS THE SYMBOL THEY ONCE USED TO SIGNIFY UNION BETWEEN A MAN AND WOMAN. HE WAS SYMBOLICALLY MAKING THEM HIS BRIDE.

YOU WILL COME TO UNDERSTAND THE GREAT ROMANCE LIKE NEVER BEFORE. YOUR LOVE WILL BE TESTED. OTHERS WILL JOIN YOU. SOME WILL LEAVE THE CIRCLE. SOME WILL DIE. ALL WILL SUFFER.

BUT IF YOU KEEP YOUR EYES ON ME UNTIL THE END, THE LAKE WILL SEEM TAME COMPARED TO WHAT AWAITS US.

WE WILL NEVER LEAVE YOU!

THEN GUARD YOUR HEART MY PRINCESS REMEMBER HOW I LOVE YOU AND LOVE ME THE SAME. ALWAYS.

BRING THEM TO ME. ALL THE DISEASED. ONE BY ONE, IF YOU MUST. SHOW THEM MY HEART. LEAD THEM INTO THE RED WATER.

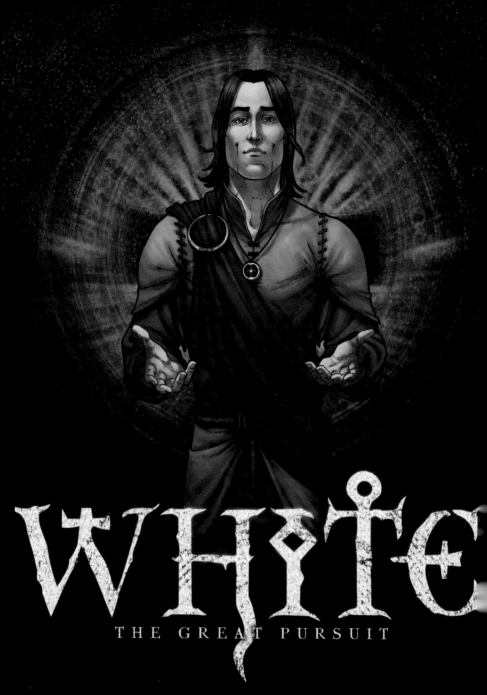

WASHINGTON D.C.

THAT WOULD BE UNDERSTATING THE MATTER, MS. JOVIC.

NO, SECRETARY GAINS, IT'S KARA HUNTER --

-- SHE SAYS IT'S URGENT.

MS. HUNTER, I'M SORRY, I REALLY DON'T HAVE TIME FOR THIS...

THOMAS!

MIKIL?

I'M...I THINK I KNOW SOMETHING ABOUT KARA...

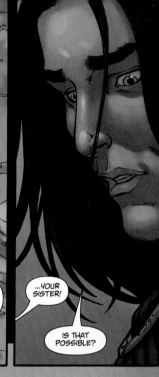

...YOUR SISTER!

IS THAT POSSIBLE?

I HAVEN'T DREAMED FOR THIRTEEN MONTHS.

DO YOU KNOW WHY?

YOU WERE KILLED IN FRANCE BY CARLOS A COUPLE DAYS AGO.

NOW MONIQUE'S MISSING, TOO, AND WE ONLY HAVE TEN DAYS TO STOP THE VIRUS.

PUT HIM ON SPEAKER.

MR. PRESIDENT?

YOU'RE ON SPEAKERPHONE, MR. HUNTER. YOUR SISTER AND MONIQUE DE RAISON ARE HERE AS WELL.

MONIQUE IS ALIVE THEN?

THE BOOK WORKS...

WHAT BOOK?

I'M SORRY, MR. PRESIDENT. KARA CAN EXPLAIN LATER. DID THE REST OF THE CIRCLE ESCAPE?

YES, THEY'RE SAFE.

WHAT'S THIS ALL ABOUT?

I KNOW THIS ISN'T MAKING A LOT OF SENSE, BUT YOU HAVE TO LISTEN. THE FRENCH WILL OFFER THE ANTIVIRUS TO ISRAEL IN AN OPEN-SEA EXCHANGE FIVE DAYS FROM NOW. THE OFFER IS GENUINE.

IF ISRAEL CALLS THEIR BLUFF AND LAUNCHES ANOTHER STRIKE, FORTIER WILL BLOW UP TEL AVIV.

YOU'RE CERTAIN OF THIS?

YES. I CAN ALSO TELL YOU FORTIER WON'T LET THE UNITED STATES SURVIVE.

CAN YOU GET ME OUT OF HERE?

I'LL HAVE GENERAL PETERS COORDINATE WITH YOU. GODSPEED, THOMAS.

THANK YOU, SIR.

SOON...

CLOSE THE PERIMETER! COVER THE EXITS! SHOOT ON SIGHT!!

THE BODY!

EEEOOOOWEEE... WEEEOOOO

THE AMERICANS HAVE STOLEN THE BODY!

UNLESS...

CHECK THE WINDOWS! SEARCH THE HOUSE! HUNTER'S BODY IS MISSING, AND I WANT IT FOUND --

NOW!

EEEOOOOOWEEEOOOOWEEEOOO

SO, THE BEAST WOREF HAS FINALLY CAUGHT THESE JACKALS.

MISTRESS CHELISE?

HE'S PARADING HIS FRUITS FOR ALL THE DAMSELS TO SEE.

EXCUSE ME, MISTRESS, BUT QURONG HAS REQUESTED YOUR PRESENCE.

DID MY FATHER SAY WHY HE WANTED TO SEE ME?

-- AND I DON'T THINK IT'S FRUIT OR FLOWERS.

ONLY THAT HE HAS A GIFT FOR YOU --

THE VILLA?

THE LIBRARY

THE ARRANGEMENT WAS SIMPLE.

CHELISE AGREED TO WAIT FOR US IN AN INNER ROOM AT DUSK.

APPARENTLY, SHE OFTEN LINGERED HERE LONG AFTER THE LIBRARIAN DEPARTED.

FREE HIS ARMS. LEAVE THE LEG CHAINS.

I DON'T HAVE ALL NIGHT, PRIEST --

-- CAN HE READ THEM OR NOT?

THIS SITUATION IS GETTING OUT OF HAND.

ONCE THE MEDIA SPREAD THE WORD ABOUT THE RAISON STRAIN, THE PROTESTS WERE INEVITABLE. THEY WANT US TO CUT A DEAL.

SO YOU'RE SAYING THAT EVEN IF WE DO FIND AN ANTIVIRUS IN THE NEXT FIVE DAYS, MANUFACTURING AND DISTRIBUTING ENOUGH MAY BE A PROBLEM?

THAT DEPENDS ON THE NATURE OF THE ANTIVIRUS, MR. PRESIDENT, BUT YOU DO UNDERSTAND THAT PEOPLE WILL DIE.

EVEN IF WE FOUND THE ANSWER TODAY -- SOME WILL DIE.

THERE IS ALSO THE LOGISTICAL PROBLEM. HOW DO YOU DELIVER THE ANTIVIRUS TO THREE HUNDRED MILLION PEOPLE IN A FEW DAYS?

WE'RE DEVELOPING THE DELIVERY SYSTEM ALREADY. THE TOOLS ARE IN PLACE.

IF WE RECEIVED THE ANTIVIRUS FROM FORTIER IN FIVE DAYS, WHEN THE FIRST SYMPTOMS APPEAR, COULD WE SAVE MOST OF OUR PEOPLE?

IF WHAT MONIQUE BELIEVES IS TRUE, WE MAY HAVE NO CHOICE.

ASSUMING THE VIRUS WAITS FIVE DAYS, AND YOU MANAGE TO CREATE A WORKABLE DELIVERY SYSTEM, YES. MOST, BUT NOT ALL.

OUR SHIPS ARE SCHEDULED TO HAND OVER OUR NUCLEAR ARSENAL IN THREE DAYS.

EVEN THEN, I DON'T TRUST FORTIER TO BE STRAIGHT WITH US OR THE ISRAELIS, FOR THAT MATTER.

OUR ONLY REAL HOPE RESTS WITH YOU, MONIQUE.

AND, PERHAPS --

-- WITH THOMAS.

KNOCK!
KNOCK!

COME.

PLEASE
FORGIVE THE
INTRUSION. QURONG
INSISTED I SPEAK
WITH YOU.

YOUR
FATHER IS
CONCERNED ABOUT
SOME MISSING
BOOKS

WHAT DO
I HAVE TO DO
WITH THIS?

I DON'T
HAVE A CLUE
WHERE THE BOOKS
COULD BE.

THE SITUATION
IS FAR MORE SERIOUS
THAN YOU KNOW. QURONG
WILL POSTPONE OUR
WEDDING UNTIL THE
BOOKS ARE FOUND.

POSTPONING
OUR WEDDING
MIGHT BE
WISE --

-- IT WOULD
GIVE YOU TIME
TO LEARN SOME
RESPECT.

TO BE HONEST, I SEE BOTH BEAUTY AND SOME THINGS WHICH AREN'T SO BEAUTIFUL.

SUCH AS?

YOUR SKIN. YOUR SCENT.

I WANTED TO BE SURE YOU WEREN'T ATTRACTED TO ME. THANKFULLY, I FIND YOU JUST AS REPELLING.

I'M SORRY. I DIDN'T MEAN... I --

--BELIEVE IT'S TIME FOR OUR LESSON.

LET'S START WITH A SIMPLE READING.

THIS IS THE WORD *THE*. DO YOU SEE IT?

NO. IT LOOKS NOTHING LIKE THE WORD *THE* TO ME.

WHAT DOES IT LOOK LIKE?

SQUIGGLY LINES.

I CAN ASSURE YOU THIS IS THE WORD *THE*. MY EYES SEE IT PLAIN AS DAY.

OH, NO...

SLAM!

YOU CAN'T LET THEM DIE, CHELISE.

IT'S OUT OF MY HANDS. HOW WOULD IT LOOK FOR ME TO BEG FOR THEIR LIVES?

WE'RE ON DEADLY GROUND HERE. I KNOW WOREF'S KIND. ONE DAY I'LL PAY FOR WHAT HE JUST SAW.

YOU HAVE TO BE MORE CAREFUL. PLEASE, KEEP YOUR DISTANCE.

I CAN DREAM NOW.

WHAT ARE YOU TALKING ABOUT?

I'VE BEEN DRINKING THE RHAMBUTAN JUICE BECAUSE THEY WOULD KILL MY FRIENDS IF I DIDN'T.

NOW, I CAN JUST REFUSE TO DRINK IT, AND I'LL DREAM TONIGHT.

PLEASE, YOU CAN'T SAY A WORD ABOUT THIS. I BEG YOU.

I...THIS ISN'T KEEPING YOUR DISTANCE.

FORGIVE ME. I LOST MY HEAD FOR A MOMENT THERE.

CLEARLY.

SO YOU'LL HELP ME?

I DON'T SEE THE HARM IN A FEW DREAMS.

AS LONG AS YOU PROMISE TO DREAM ABOUT ME.

PHIL GRANT.

FATHER, HUSBAND, CIA DIRECTOR...

...TRAITOR.

WELL, SPEAK OF THE DEVIL!

WE'RE DOWN TO THE WIRE, DWIGHT. IF YOU CAN'T "INSPIRE" THIS CROWD, THE PRESIDENT'S GOING TO DO SOMETHING STUPID.

YOU'RE NOT SAYING HE'D START A WAR. NOT NOW.

I -- I'LL SEE WHAT I CAN DO.

YOU DO THAT.

THAT'S EXACTLY WHAT I'M SAYING! HE'S CONVINCED THAT FRANCE WON'T DELIVER THE ANTIVIRUS, AND HE'S DECIDED TO GO DOWN IN FLAMES.

AND TAKE THE WHOLE BLASTED COUNTRY WITH HIM?! WE'RE ALL GOING TO DIE, DWIGHT!!

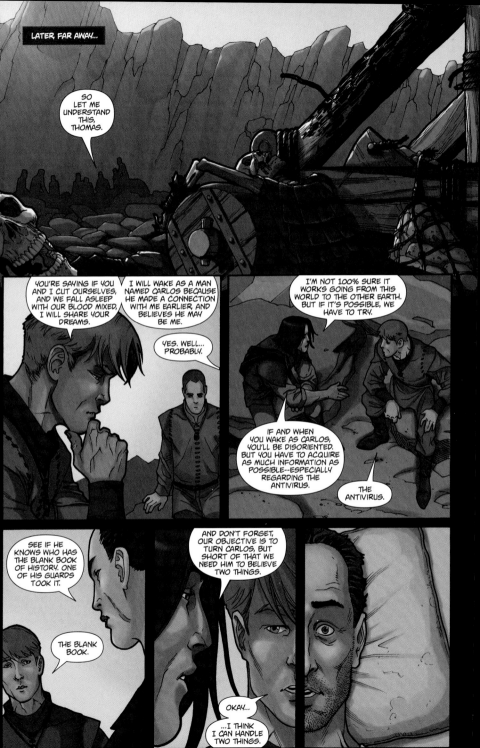

I'M IN THE DREAM THOMAS SPOKE OF.

DOES CARLOS REALIZE I'M HERE?

HUNTER...?

NO, IT'S ME. JOHAN. I KNOW HIS THOUGHTS, BUT HE DOESN'T KNOW MINE. NOT YET, ANYWAY.

CARLOS ISN'T THE ONE DREAMING. I AM. IT'S JUST AS THOMAS SAID IT WOULD BE.

NO ONE. AM I SO PARANOID?

THIS IS HOW YOU'LL FEEL WHEN FORTIER SLIPS POISON INTO YOUR DRINK AFTER HE'S PLAYED YOU FOR A FOOL.

WHY WOULD FORTIER LET ANYONE CAPABLE OF A COUP LIVE? YOU HAVE A DAY, AT THE MOST. THEN HE WILL SNUFF YOU OUT.

HE MIGHT EVEN TAKE CARE OF YOU NOW.

CARLOS, PLEASE JOIN ME IN THE MAP ROOM.

AND THERE'S SOMETHING ABOUT A BOOK OF NAMES. THE FRENCHMAN IS PLANNING SOMETHING NO ONE EXPECTS.

SOMETHING ABOUT THE PEOPLE HE PLANS TO GIVE THE ANTIVIRUS TO. IT'S FAR FEWER THAN EVERYONE THINKS.

I KNEW IT! I --

THOMAS, YOU HAVE COMPANY!

WE FOUND HIM, ALONE, WANDERING IN THE DESERT.

I- I AM UNARMED. MY ONLY PURPOSE IS TO TAKE YOUR RESPONSE BACK TO COMMANDER WOREF.

AND TO WHAT AM I REPLYING?

WHY WOULD THEY THINK SUCH AN ABSURD DEMAND WOULD BE OF ANY CONCERN TO US?

TELL ME ABOUT CARLOS'S PLANS. DO YOU THINK HE CAN BE TURNED?

MAYBE. HE'S ALREADY GIVEN TO SUPERNATURAL IDEAS.

QURONG HAS DECLARED THAT UNLESS YOU RETURN IN THREE DAYS, HE WILL DROWN HIS DAUGHTER, CHELISE, FOR TREASON.

SHE ALLOWED ME TO DREAM...

I CALL A COUNCIL. A WOMAN'S LIFE IS AT STAKE.

WHAT'S WRONG WITH ME? SHE'S A SCAB COVERED BY DISEASE.

HER BREATH SMELLS LIKE SULFUR. HER MIND CLOUDED BY DECEPTION.

THEN WHY THIS INEXORABLE ATTRACTION TO HER?

WHY CAN I NOT REMOVE HER FROM MY MIND?

WHY AM I HAUNTED BY HER FACE --

-- EVERYWHERE I TURN?

HELLO, THOMAS.

OVER HERE, OLD FRIEND.

THOMAS, WAKE UP.

WHERE AM I?

THE WHITE HOUSE. PRESIDENT BLAIR'S WAITING FOR US.

WE'VE HAD RIOTS IN SEVENTEEN CITIES, AND THE VIRUS HAS ALREADY STARTED TO SHOW ITSELF.

THE *SYMPTOMS*, YOU MEAN? I THOUGHT WE HAD AT LEAST *FIVE* DAYS.

WE WERE WRONG.

KARA TOLD ME IT WORKED, THAT YOUR MAN DREAMED AS CARLOS.

YES-- AND I'M CERTAIN FORTIER WON'T GIVE US AN ANTIVIRUS THAT WORKS. THE NUMBER OF SURVIVORS WILL ALSO BE SMALLER THAN ANYONE IMAGINES.

OUR ONLY VIABLE SHOT AT THE ANTIVIRUS IS IF I CAN WIN CARLOS OVER.

OKAY, BUT WE'RE RUNNING OUT OF TIME.

THEN GET ME TO FRANCE.

THIRTY MINUTES LATER

TOO EASY.

THE GOGGLES!

I SEE YOU INSIST ON HOUNDING ME UNTIL I KILL YOU FOR GOOD.

CARLOS.

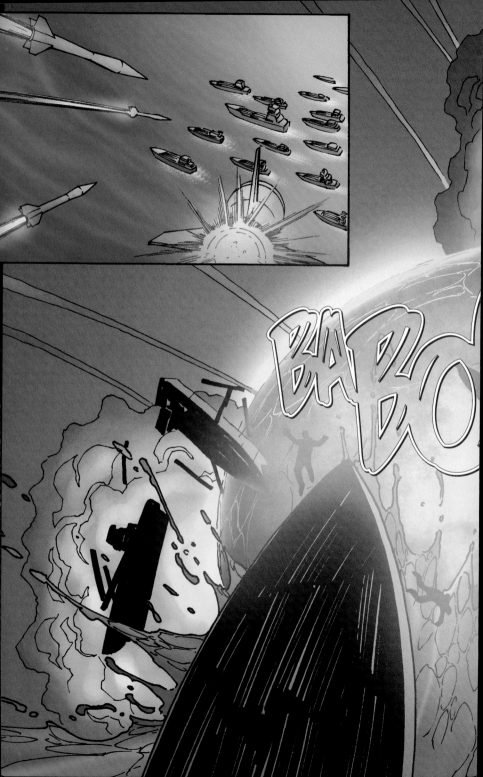

THE MIGHTY THOMAS OF HUNTER. SO CLEVER, SO BRAVE. TO COME ALL THIS WAY FOR NOTHING.

WILLIAM IS DEAD.

WILLIAM?

YOU REMEMBER-- TALL, GREEN EYES, TALKS TOO MUCH. HE CONVINCED ME TO SPARE THE TRIBE IN EXCHANGE FOR YOU. SUCH A NOBLE SACRIFICE...

...ALL FOR NOTHING.

NO.

IT WASN'T FOR NOTHING. HE BOUGHT THE LIFE OF THE CIRCLE WITH HIS OWN BLOOD.

AND ARE YOU SO HEROIC? WOULD YOU SACRIFICE YOUR LIFE--YOUR LOVE--TO SAVE CHELISE?

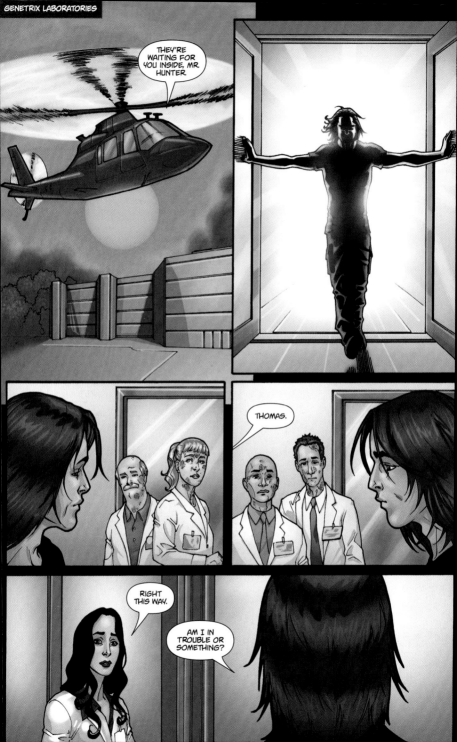

NO, THAT WOULD BE THE *FORMER* DIRECTOR OF THE CIA. YOU'RE BEYOND REPROACH AS FAR AS I'M CONCERNED.

HARDLY.

WE'VE FOUND SOMETHING, THOMAS. IT COULD BE VERY GOOD. AND IT COULD ALSO BE VERY BAD. YOU SEE --

-- YOU'RE VIRUS-FREE, THOMAS.

I'VE RUN YOUR BLOOD THROUGH EVERY TEST I COULD THINK OF.

IT KILLED THE VIRUS IN A MATTER OF MINUTES.

I'M... IMMUNE?

MONIQUE AND I WERE ALSO IN CONTACT WITH YOUR BLOOD. IT KILLED THE VIRUS IN US AS WELL.

I THINK IT WAS THE LAKE. YOU WERE HEALED IN ELYON'S WATER, AND IT CHANGED YOUR BLOOD.

DO YOU KNOW WHAT IT IS ABOUT MY BLOOD THAT KILLS THE VIRUS?

NOT ENTIRELY, BUT ENOUGH TO DUPLICATE IT, YES. WE HAVE BEEN ABLE TO ADD IT TO A COMPOUND WHICH REPLICATES THE ANTIVIRAL EFFECTS OF--

I DON'T CARE ABOUT THE SCIENCE. JUST CUT TO THE BOTTOM LINE. YOU NEED MY BLOOD. HOW MUCH?

"WE CAN, HOWEVER, STRIVE TO LIVE OUR LIVES IN A MANNER WORTHY OF HIS LIFE."

"FOR A PORTION OF THAT LIFE NOW LIVES WITHIN US ALL."

"MAY IT BRING OUT THE BEST IN EACH OF US."

"AND MAY GOD BLESS YOU ALL."

IT...IT WAS LOVELY.

SO STRANGE, THOUGH. I MEAN, HE'S STILL ALIVE. NOT HERE, BUT IN HIS DREAM WORLD.

THERE IS SOMETHING THAT WORRIES ME, THOUGH.

THE BLANK BOOK.

YES.

YES. SOMEWHERE IN THE WORLD IS ONE BOOK, MAYBE MORE, WITH MORE POWER THAN ALL THE NUCLEAR WEAPONS THAT WERE SUNK.

SURELY IT WILL SHOW UP.

THAT'S WHAT I'M AFRAID OF.

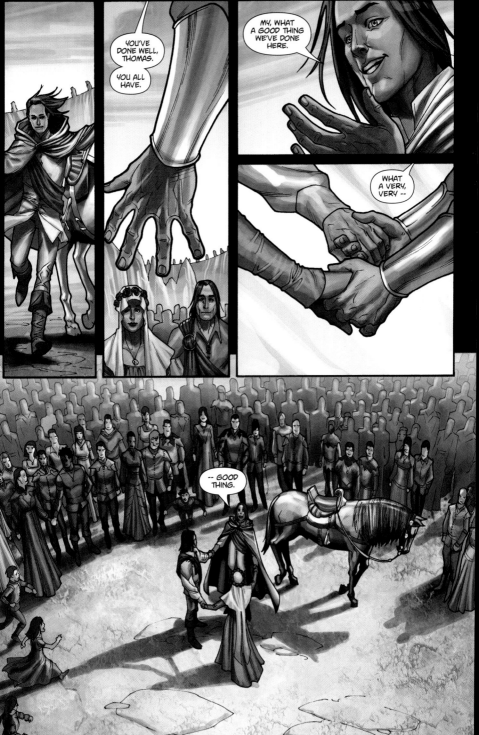

Written by: Ted Dekker

Adapted by:

    Black: Matt Hansen and Bob Strachan

    Red: Matt Hansen

    White: J.S. Earls and Mike S. Miller

Colors by:

    Black: Big Jack Studios: Jose Carlos, Giovanna Guimaraes, and Alex Starling

    Red: Big Jack Studios: Giovanna Guimaraes, Eber Ferreira, Jose Carlos, and Gulliver Vianei

    White: "Our World": David Curiel (additional colors: Josh Burcham and Imaginary Friends Studios); "Other World": Imaginary Friends Studios

Lettered by:

    Black: Matt Moylan and Bill Tortolini

    Red and *White*: Bill Tortolini

Art by:

    Black: Big Jack Studios: Ig Barros, Eduardo Pansica, and Ricardo Ratton

    Red: Jack Studios: Ricardo Ratton, Eduardo Pansica, and Newton Barbosa

    White: Mike S. Miller

Edited by:

    Black and *Red*: Kevin Kaiser

    White: Mike S. Miller and Kevin Kaiser

Original Graphic Novel Cover Art by: Mike S. Miller (*White* cover colors by Imaginary Friends Studios)

Published in Nashville, Tennessee, by Thomas Nelson. Thomas Nelson is a registered trademark of Thomas Nelson, Inc.

Thomas Nelson, Inc., titles may be purchased in bulk for educational, business, fund-raising, or sales promotional use. For information, please e-mail SpecialMarkets@ThomasNelson.com.

ISBN 978-1-59554-858-0 (Visual Edition)

Library of Congress Cataloging-in-Publication Data

Hansen, Matthew.
   Black : graphic novel / written by Ted Dekker ; adapted by Matthew Hansen & Bob Strachan ; edited by Kevin Kaiser.
     p. cm. — (The circle trilogy ; bk. 1)
   Includes bibliographical references and index.
   ISBN 0-9795900-0-0 (pbk. : alk. paper) 1. Graphic novels. I. Strachan, Bob. II. Kaiser, Kevin. III. Dekker, Ted, 1962- Black. IV. Title.
  PN6733.H36B53 2008
  741.5'973—dc22   200705040

Hansen, Matthew.
   Red : graphic novel / written by Ted Dekker ; adapted by Matthew Hansen; edited by Kevin Kaiser & Bob Strachan.
     p. cm. — (The circle trilogy ; bk. 2)
   Graphic novel adaptation of Red by Ted Dekker.
   Includes bibliographical references and index.
   ISBN 978-0-9795900-1-6 (pbk. : alk. paper) 1. Graphic novels. I. Kaiser, Kevin. II. Strachan, Bob. III. Dekker, Ted, 1962– Red. IV. Title.
  PN6733.H36R44 2008
  741.5'973—dc22   2007050415

Earls, J.S.
   White : the great pursuit : a graphic novel / Ted Dekker ; adapted by J.S. Earls and Mike S. Miller ; edited by Mike S. Miller, Kevin Kaiser.
     p. cm. — (The Circle Trilogy ; bk. 3)
   Graphic novel adaptation of White by Ted Dekker
   Includes bibliographical references and index
   ISBN 978-0-979500-2-3 (pbk. : alk paper)
   1. Graphic novels I. Kaiser, Kevin. II. Miller, Mike S. III. Dekker, Ted, 1962– White. IV. Title.
  PN6733.E27W45 2007
  741.5'973—dc22   2007050418

Printed in the United States of America

09 10 11 12 13 WC 5 4 3 2 1

GO
FULL CIRCLE

Discover the Lost Books Graphic Novels

NOTHER TIME AND PLACE.

ON A STRANGELY FAMILIAR, YET UTTERLY DIFFERENT WORLD.

A WORLD WHERE -- THOUSANDS OF YEARS FROM NOW -- OUR OWN HISTORY APPEARS TO BE REPEATING ITSELF.

MAGNIFICENT FORESTS OF MANY COLORS ONCE COVERED THIS WORLD.

ITS PEOPLE LIVING IN PERFECT HARMONY WITH ELYON, THEIR LOVING CREATOR.

THEN CAME THE DARKNESS.

TEELEH, THE WICKED ONE, DECEIVED MANKIND, AND THE GREAT FORESTS WERE SOON WITHERING INTO DESERT WASTELANDS.

THE POWERFUL GREEN WATERS, ONCE PRECIOUS TO ELYON, HAVE ALL BUT VANISHED FROM THE EARTH. ONLY SEVEN SMALL LAKES IN SEVEN SMALL FORESTS REMAIN.

EVIL NOW RULES THE WORLD, REVEALING ITSELF IN THE PAINFUL, SCALY DISEASE COVERING THE DESERT-DWELLERS KNOWN AS THE HORDE.

THE FEW FOLLOWERS OF ELYON WHO REMAIN NOW LIVE IN THE FORESTS, BATHING DAILY IN THE HEALING WATERS TO WASH AWAY THE CURSED DISEASE.

FEARING THE GREEN WATERS ABOVE ALL ELSE, THEIR ENEMY -- THE HORDE -- HAVE SWORN TO WIPE ALL TRACES OF THE FORESTS FROM THE FACE OF THE PLANET.

ONLY THE FOREST GUARD STANDS IN THEIR WAY. BUT THE GUARD IS STARTING TO CRUMBLE.

ENDLESS WAR HAS DEVASTATED THE RANKS OF THE GUARD, FORCING THEIR LEADER -- THE LEGENDARY THOMAS HUNTER -- TO FIND EVEN YOUNGER RECRUITS.

FROM AMONG THESE ONE THOUSAND NEW RECRUITS, ONLY FOUR MAY BECOME LEADERS.

ONLY FOUR SHALL BE --

WHAT DO YOU SAY, JOHNIS? WHO'S THE STRONGEST?

DARSAL.

NOW THERE'S A CHOICE. SHE'D MAKE ANY MAN A FINE WIFE.

THE BALL!

THEY'RE SO BUSY FIGHTING, THEY DON'T EVEN SEE IT.

EVERYONE IN THE STADIUM KNOWS WHERE IT IS, EXCEPT FOR THOSE VIOLENT BRUTES.

SOMEONE SHOULD SAY SOMETHING. LET THEM KNOW WHERE IT IS.

A LITTLE MORE MUSCLE ON THOSE BONES AND YOU COULD MAKE A PLAY FOR HER YET, BOY.

I SUPPOSE, I --

THOUGH SHE DOES SEEM A BIT TAKEN WITH THAT OTHER BOY...

WHAT AM I THINKING?

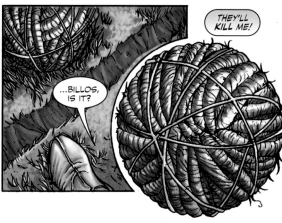

...BILLOS, IS IT?

THEY'LL KILL ME!

STOP!

CURSED HORDE BALL.

MADE FROM THE HAIR OF THE BEASTS WHO MURDERED MY MOTHER.

CAN'T BEAR TO LOOK AT IT.

BOTH TEAMS ON YOUR FEET!

AREN'T YOU ALL FORGETTING SOMETHING? THE GOAL ISN'T TO BEAT ONE ANOTHER INTO BLOODY PULPS.

IT'S TO GET THE HORDE BALL AND GET IT OVER THE GOAL LINE!